Take No Prisoners

Also by Monty R. Garner

Buckshot

Card Jordan Series

Card, Kill Them All

Card, Man of Justice

Card, Taking Care of Business

Card, Day of Reckoning

Card, Duty Calls

Card, Unleashed

Card, A Test of Faith

Sawyer McCade Series

Life After War

Take No Prisoners

Sawyer McCade
Book 2

Monty R. Garner

WOLFPACK
PUBLISHING
— EST 2013 —

Take No Prisoners

Chapter One

It was a beautiful August day, and a crowd of townspeople stood on the courthouse lawn in Humboldt, Kansas, waiting for an adjoining-county judge to arrive for the swearing-in ceremony of their newly elected sheriff.

The county residents had banded together to elect ex-soldier and hometown boy, Sawyer McCade, as their next chief law officer.

Sawyer stood alone at the window inside an empty judge's office, in awe of the size of the crowd that had assembled.

Even though that part of Kansas was partial to the Union, Sawyer had fought for the Confederate States. He'd anticipated some hard feelings from the townsfolk when he returned home from fighting for the South, but they had come out in masses to elect him as their new sheriff.

Standing there in exuberance and appreciation gave him time to reflect on his life. Never had he imagined he would end up as a lawman. When the Civil War ended, the long trip home after he left his regiment in Arkansas had given him time to consider his options and do some much-needed soul searching. Spending three years away from home fighting for his life on the battlefield instilled in him the hankering to reunite with his family. With renewed hope, he had intended to return home and help his parents work the family farm. Although he hated farming, it was something he felt he should do to help his parents.

But all that changed when he arrived in Humboldt and learned that his mother and father had been murdered seven months earlier, and the bank had foreclosed on their land. Even hard men had moments of sorrow and despair, and this had been one of those times for Sawyer.

What had happened to his parents wasn't an isolated incident. He'd thought long and hard about what to do about the murdering of innocent folks and the crooks taking their land. After surveying the situation, he decided not to get involved in what was happening because the last thing he wanted was to be pulled into another war. So instead of staying and getting revenge, he took his army companions up on their invitation to gather wild longhorns in Texas and start ranching. He and his friends had been ready to begin their journey from Clarksville, Texas, to the pine and mesquite thickets of southeast Texas, but before they could leave, he was summoned back to Humboldt at his sister Nancy Lou's request.

His sister was his only living relative now, and she needed his help. Her husband had been murdered, and she feared for her life and her unborn child because the crooks were still active, and they wanted more land.

He couldn't ignore his sister's plea. He had to go back home and confront the men responsible for the murders of his parents and brother-in-law. He left Texas that fearful day when he received the request for help. He knew that he would have to revert to his army training—he would not spare any compassion for the men he was going after.

The seven-day trip back to Kansas had given him plenty of time to develop his plan and put him in the right state of mind to tackle the hardened criminals who were taking over people's farms. And now here he was, becoming sheriff.

The acknowledgment that the men of his hometown had elected him to the office of sheriff put a smile on his face. Even though the women couldn't vote, they stood beside their husbands. The good people of Allen County trusted him, and he would soon take an oath to uphold the law and serve the people. But things could change quickly, and dreams often faded like the setting sun. He had dreamed of becoming a rancher. He had never dreamed of becoming a lawman. Now he was about to take on that critical responsibility in just a few minutes.

The court clerk interrupted Sawyer's thoughts when she opened the door and said, "Sheriff, the judge is here to swear you in."

"Thank you! I'll be right out." As he took one last look out the window at the courthouse lawn where the townspeople had gathered, he saw the judge in his robe, as well as Reverend Toliver and Nancy Lou standing in front of the steps waiting on him. Sawyer made his way to a mirror that hung from the wall. He looked into the pale blue eyes of a hardened twenty-three-year-old

3

warrior. He smiled at his clean-shaven face and hand-some good looks before making sure there wasn't any food stuck between his teeth that someone might see. He took a deep breath, blew himself a kiss, and went outside.

The man of the hour came down the courthouse steps to be greeted by Reverend Toliver. "Sawyer, this is Judge Lee from Wilson County."

Sawyer stuck out his hand. "I'm pleased to meet you, Judge. I'm sorry that you had to come all this way today."

"It's my pleasure. I've heard many good things about you, and you'll make a fine sheriff."

"Thank you, sir."

"Let's get the ceremony started, shall we?" The judge turned to the crowd. "I would appreciate it if you would be silent until the swearing-in oath is finished. Reverend Toliver will use his Bible today, and he and Nancy Lou will be our witnesses."

Sawyer took his place next to the preacher.

"Sawyer," said the judge, "place your right hand on the Bible and repeat after me. 'I, Sawyer McCade, do solemnly swear that I will support, obey, and defend the Constitution of the United States and the Constitution of the State of Kansas and that I will not knowingly receive, directly or indirectly, any money or other valu-ables like land, liquor, horses and women, so help me God.'"

Sawyer repeated the words, and Judge Lee handed Nancy Lou the badge.

"Would you be so kind as to pin this badge on your brother?" he asked her.

"It will be my honor. Thank you, Judge." She placed the badge on her brother's vest and hugged him.

The judge turned to the crowd. "I now present to you, Sheriff Sawyer McCade."

Sawyer waved at the onlookers with both hands while the townspeople clapped and cheered.

When the applause stopped, he turned to the judge and shook his hand. "Thanks again for coming all this way."

"It's been an honor to be here today. But if you'll excuse me, I have to get going." He turned to Reverend Toliver. "It was good to see you again, preacher."

"Don't be a stranger—come back any time," said the reverend.

Sawyer took a few steps toward the townspeople. "Folks, I want to thank you all for voting for me, and I promise to uphold the law to the best of my abilities."

The crowd offered words of encouragement as Sawyer made his way through the throng, shaking everyone's hands and thanking them for coming out.

When he eventually made his rounds through the crowd, he returned to where Reverend Toliver and Nancy stood. Sawyer gave the preacher a hug. "Thank you so much for being our friend. It means the world to me. I think me and Nancy Lou will head on out of here. I have a big day planned tomorrow."

"You two go on home," said the reverend, patting Sawyer on the back. "I'm proud of the man you're striving to become."

It took close to ten minutes for Sawyer to get away from the courthouse lawn and for the host of residents to disperse. He was filled with pride and admiration with the great turnout and support, thanks to the citizens of Humboldt.

Today marked a new chapter in his life, and he would do his best to serve and fulfill the promises he had made about getting rid of crime in their town.

He took hold of his sister's arm. "Let's go to the café and celebrate over a steak. I'm buying."

"That sounds good to me! I didn't want to cook tonight, and this baby needs food." She rubbed her growing belly and grinned.

Sawyer smiled too. In six months, he would be an uncle.

She stopped on the boardwalk. "Sawyer, it's a blessing to have you as my brother. I wish Mama, Papa, and Richard could have been here to see the ceremony today. I miss them every day. I wasn't sure I'd survive without Richard, but you being home again has given me a new outlook on life."

Sawyer had to bend over to hug his sister since she was only five foot six and he was six foot three. "Being here with you has given me a new outlook on life also, and I can't wait until your baby is born so I can spoil it. I love you."

She took time to wipe the tears off her face before she put her arm in his, and they continued to the café.

After supper, they decided to rent rooms at the hotel since it was late and they didn't want to ride the three miles to Nancy's house in the country. On their way to the hotel, they saw Deputy Craig Martin across the street, lighting a streetlamp. "You go on to the hotel. I need to talk to Craig for a few minutes," said Sawyer.

"Hello, how are you this evening?" he called out as he walked toward Craig.

"I'm good, Sheriff."

"I'd like you to stay on as a deputy, but with a few conditions," Sawyer said. "You'll have to be honest in all your dealings, uphold the law, and serve the people in the county."

Craig extended his hand. "I can do that, and it'll be a pleasure to work for you."

"Thanks, Deputy. I'll see you in the morning." Sawyer shook the man's hand and headed to the hotel for the night.

Chapter Two

Rufus Sanger and Avery O'Neil arrived in Humboldt, Kansas, on the afternoon of August 2, 1865—the day before the election for sheriff. They came into town on the stagecoach, dressed in cheap, worn suits and bowler hats. As they traveled, they minded their own business and didn't talk to the other passengers. They had been sent to Humboldt by their boss, US Senator Alfred T. Bass, with the orders to lay low and observe the other men in town who worked for him, since he wanted to know how his criminal enterprises in Allen County were operating. It just so happened that they shared the same stagecoach into town with the two men they were sent to watch: Nathaniel Hopson and Howard McMillan.

Rufus had met with Senator Bass in Kansas City a week earlier to review his assignment since the senator wasn't pleased with some of the things that had happened in Humboldt lately.

The senator had informed Rufus that he had six hired guns in Humboldt on his payroll, as well as

Nathaniel and Howard, and the sheriff and county judge. Rufus was to gather what information he could about what the men were up to, and report back to the senator without getting found out.

Rufus kept most of the details to himself, only telling his associate in crime, Avery, the bare minimum. Avery lacked intelligence but made up for it with his ability to follow the most brutal orders and commit crimes.

When they arrived in Humboldt, Rufus and Avery were the last two men to exit the stage. Rufus said to Avery, "Get our bags and meet me at the hotel." He pointed to the north.

"Okay. Are you going to check us into rooms?" asked Avery.

Rufus shook his head, dismayed since he had just told him to come to the hotel. "Just get the bags and follow me. Can you do that without asking any more stupid questions?"

Rufus was still shaking his head at his dimwitted associate as he hurried down the boardwalk. Upon arriving at the hotel check-in counter, he said, "I'd like two rooms that face the street for a week."

The hotel clerk pushed the ledger in front of his new guest and turned to get the keys. Rufus signed the book as John Brown and laid the pen on the counter.

"Y'all will be in rooms ten and twelve. That will be forty-two dollars for a week. We also have a dining room through those doors to your left."

"Thanks." Rufus counted out the money and handed it to the clerk before picking up the keys.

Avery came through the doors with the two bags, and Rufus motioned for him to follow him upstairs.

When they were in the upstairs hallway, both men took their bags and went to their separate rooms. A few minutes later, Rufus knocked on Avery's door. Rufus still wore his suit clothes but had a gun holstered on his hip. "Let's go walk around town and get a lay of the businesses we're supposed to observe. Then we'll come back here and take turns watching them from our room windows."

"If anyone asks, what're we here for, anyway?" asked Avery.

"I've already told you this twice. We're business-people looking into selling seeds and fertilizer to farmers around here. That should be all anyone needs to know, so don't shoot off your mouth," exclaimed Rufus. He had to watch Avery constantly so he didn't do or say something stupid that would draw attention to them.

The two men left the hotel, and Rufus explained their mission to Avery as they walked. "The bank is one of our main focuses to keep an eye on. The other important point will be the McMillan Land Office, then the Star Saloon, Adams Mercantile, the newspaper, and finally the telegraph office. The man who runs the bank was one of the young fellers on the stage with us. His name is Nathaniel Hopson. The other man was Howard McMillan, and he runs the land office. Our jobs are to observe them and how the townspeople spend their money with them. We have to watch without them knowing what we're doing."

"Can we go into the saloon we're supposed to watch and check it out from the inside?" asked Avery.

"No! I want you sober so you don't draw attention

to us. There'll be no liquor until we have what we need for our boss," said Rufus in a hateful tone.

"Okay, you don't have to get huffy about it."

"There are six hired guns 'round here that work for our boss, but I don't know who they are. So we'll split up and see if we can talk with a few people to find out who these men are and what they look like," said Rufus. "Be careful and don't let on why you're asking, and I'll meet you in the hotel lobby at five thirty."

Rufus went to the first mercantile he came to and picked himself out a new shirt, a pair of socks, and a comb for his hair. As he paid for his things, he casually said, "I may be speaking out of turn, but I've seen quite a few men with guns that I suspect are hired gunfighters around here."

The clerk continued to wrap Rufus's items in brown paper. When he had finished tying twine around the package, he said, "You be careful what you say and what you ask in town. Those men work for Nathaniel Hopson and stay at the Star Saloon. I wouldn't go near that place if I were you."

"That's good to know. I'll watch who I talk to while I'm here."

Rufus strolled along the boardwalk observing people, tipping his hat to the ladies but keeping a watchful eye on the saloon. He thought back to the stage station when he and Avery had arrived. Two men in suits had met Nathaniel and Howard and exchanged bags with the stage driver. Now all he had to do was figure out the identity of the other four gunmen.

A leisurely stroll by the saloon, where he peeked into the large room through the front windows, proved beneficial. He saw the bartender talking to a well-dressed man who carried a ledger and left through a door behind the bar area. Three other men were at a table drinking beer and playing cards. One of the men he recognized as Fargo, a man who hired out his gun to whoever paid the most. Rufus smiled since he knew how the man operated and went on his merry way.

After dark, the two men sat in Rufus's hotel room and watched the street. Rufus filled Avery in on what he had learned about the hired gunmen, and Avery also had some news to share. Two of the men were a couple of fellers Avery had heard of. They were Lefty Branch and Lesley Overstreet. Lefty wore a two-gun rig but was right-handed, which was an important thing to know.

"Good work, Avery, for finding out about those two hard cases," said Rufus.

They watched as the men they were supposed to spy on went into the saloon. Rufus quickly noticed that the only ones going into the drinking hole were the men they were to observe and their hired guns. No local drinkers were using the Star Saloon, that he could tell. Instead, it appeared that the locals were spending their money in other establishments. He pulled a leather-bound notepad from his bag and wrote something in it. It could be information the senator needed to know, since the saloon wasn't making any money off the town.

Around nine that night, Rufus got up from his chair and walked toward the bed. "It's getting late, and I'm tired. Go on to your room, and I'll meet you for breakfast in the morning."

"That's a good idea. I'm also tired. That stage ride wore me out." Avery stood about halfway out of the chair before he sat back down. "Hey, Rufus, here comes someone walking to the Star Saloon, and I ain't seen him before."

"Maybe it's just a local going for a drink."

"Don't think so. He just pulled both of his guns and is standing outside the door," said Avery.

"What! Let me see." Rufus ran to the window in time to see the man go inside.

Rufus and Avery heard multiple rounds of gunfire coming from inside the saloon. They could see the light flashes through the windows each time a shot was fired. Finally, smoke from all the gunpowder began plowing through the air above the batwing doors.

"This ain't goin' to be good. I counted fourteen shots, and it seems like it's over with now," said Avery, shaking his head.

They both stuck their heads out the open window to try to see what had happened.

Less than a minute later, Rufus pointed toward the bar. "Here comes that feller you saw with his guns still drawn. It looks like he's headed up the street to kill someone else," said Rufus.

"Do we need to confront him outside?" asked Avery.

Rufus looked at Avery. "Are you stupid enough to confront a man with two guns who just took on a half dozen hired gun hands and lived to see another day?"

Avery made a face like he was in deep thought. "I see your point. Look!" he said, pointing out the window. "Here comes that McMillan feller who was on the stage with us and another man out of the upstairs door at the land office."

When the shooting started up again, Rufus and Avery pulled their heads back inside the room. By the time they stuck their heads back out the window again, the shooting had stopped, the gunman had killed McMillan and his companion. Rufus and Avery watched as the shooter checked to ensure that both men were dead. Then he started back up the street toward the saloon but turned toward the sheriff's office.

"What's he doing now?" asked Rufus.

"Rufus, look at the sheriff." Avery pointed. "He came out of his office and is running down the street away from town. I don't think he wants anything to do with that gunman."

"Yeah, that figures. The sheriff and the county judge both work for our boss. I'm sure he's assuming that Hopson and McMillan are dead. He's scared, with his tail between his legs and running away," said Rufus.

"What? Now you're telling me there ain't no law in town, and we can do whatever we want?"

"No, we'll do what our boss tells us to do and nothing else," said Rufus, getting aggravated at Avery. "I've got to go to the telegraph office and notify the boss of what's happened, but first I need some answers. So you come with me, and we'll see if we can find out who the shooter is and make sure he killed all of them."

"Sure thing, boss. I'm kind of curious to see if he did kill everyone in the saloon," said Avery.

Rufus and Avery hurried to the saloon, where they looked in the windows to see the undertaker going from corpse to corpse to ensure the men were dead.

"Avery, stay out in the street and start asking the men gathering in the street who the shooter is, and I'll go inside."

Rufus made his way past some onlookers who were standing on the boardwalk trying to peer through the batwing doors so he could get a good look at the carnage that had taken place. He had to step around one body lying on the floor between him and the undertaker.

He went to the undertaker and asked, "What in the Sam Hill happened tonight, and who was that gun hand?"

"That was Sawyer McCade. He'll be our new sheriff tomorrow after the election. These men killed his family and brother-in-law, he doesn't dillydally around regarding revenge."

Rufus went back outside and motioned for Avery to come to him. "You go to the saloon down the street, have one drink and listen to what's said about the shooting and the man who did it. Then go to the hotel and wait on me."

Rufus went to the telegraph office and hit the door with his shoulder hard enough to jar the lock off the facing. He knew how to send and receive messages himself—years ago, he'd worked as a telegraph operator.

Urgent Message to Senator Bass, Kansas City, Missouri.

The newly elected sheriff, Sawyer McCade, killed the entire crew, Hopson and McMillan, dead. Sheriff Kiser left town. I don't know about the judge. Waiting for instructions.

Rufus sat down at the operator's desk and waited, hoping the senator would get the message quickly and send a reply. Senator Bass had been his employer for the past ten years, and Rufus knew he was a shrewd businessman who understood when it was time to cut his losses and leave town.

Rufus was snoring when the telegraph key began to tap. He wrote down the message and acknowledged that he had received the reply from his boss.

Take my money from the bank. Eliminate the judge and the old sheriff.

Rufus read the message a second time before he put the paper in his pocket and left the telegraph office, heading across the street to the hotel.

When he got to his room, Rufus found Avery lying on his bed, almost asleep. "Get off my bed," said Rufus, grabbing Avery's legs and shoving them off the mattress. "Come on, we have to find where the judge lives and if he has a hideout when there's trouble," said Rufus.

The two men spent two hours asking questions at the livery stable, the saloon, and of a few people who were still in the diner. Rufus finally learned that the judge owned a farm out in the country east of town. They went back to the hotel to get some sleep, the next day would be a long one.

The following morning, Rufus purchased horses and saddles from the livery stable for the two of them. Without anything to do because they had to rob the bank tonight before they could leave town, the two men ate a late noon meal and walked around the bank building, casing it. Rufus read a notice nailed to the front door of the bank. It notified the town that it would be closed until a new owner was found. Rufus saw people standing on the courthouse lawn and motioned for Avery to follow him to see what was happening. They were in the crowd in front of the courthouse when Sawyer announced that the bank would reopen tomorrow and be operated by his sister, since the bank had been closed for a day. The previous owner was a crook and no longer alive.

Rufus touched Avery on the arm. "Let's go. We have work to do."

When they were back at the hotel, Rufus said, "Change into your range clothes because tonight we're breaking into the bank and taking our boss's money before it opens tomorrow. Then we're goin' to find that judge's farm and kill him."

"Do we get to keep the money we steal from the bank?"

"No, you idiot, it belongs to our boss. He would have both of us killed if we kept it."

"What time do you want to break into the bank?"

"We'll get a few hours of sleep and then steal that crowbar I saw leaning against the wall at the livery stable earlier. I'm thinking if we leave the hotel at eleven, most people will be asleep and we won't be seen," said Rufus.

"Fine by me. I'm going to my room till then," said Avery.

Chapter Three

On his first official day as sheriff, Sawyer woke early. After he finished shaving and getting dressed for the day, he sat in his hotel room and thought about how quickly life could change. The night before election day, he had single-handedly killed the criminals who had been stealing land and murdering the good people who wouldn't sell their property.

Sawyer was elected because he'd uncovered a scandal that had rocked the entire county. Nathaniel Hopson, the bank president, had been in cahoots with Howard McMillan, who owned the local land company. The two men had come to Humboldt during the Civil War, beginning their reign of terror against helpless farmers who couldn't protect themselves. Unfortunately, the ex-sheriff and the county judge had also been on Hopson and McMillan's payroll.

The whirlwind of events over the last month had almost made him forget about the horrors of war he had experienced over the previous three years. Finally, this day would be the beginning of his new job, and he'd be able to put all the pieces together. He and Nancy Lou would be able to start returning the deeds to people whose land had been robbed from them. But there might be more obstacles ahead for the inexperienced young sheriff. First, he would have to learn to be a lawman and not react in a hostile manner when threatened.

Sawyer walked through the door of the sheriff's office and smelled coffee. On the potbelly stove between the door and the jail cells sat a pot of freshly brewed java. He breathed deeply and paused to take it all in. To his right were two chairs and a hall tree for coats. In the middle of the room were his desk and chair, and two more chairs for guests sat in front of the desk. The left side of the office was divided into cells to house prisoners.

Craig was sweeping the floor in front of the cells. "Good morning, Deputy," said Sawyer.

"Good morning, Sheriff. I take it you spent the night in town?"

"Yeah. How about you put that broom away and let's have a cup and talk about what I want to accomplish today?" Sawyer poured two cups of the steaming hot morning joe, and he and Craig sat down.

"The first thing on my list is to go through everything in the jail and throw away anything that belonged to Kiser."

"That won't take much time. He ain't got much stuff here. It's mostly in cell one—he used it as his away-from-home bed."

"Good, we'll get that cleaned out and then go to the land office. It might take a while to search for evidence of McMillan stealing people's property."

"Okay," said the deputy as he blew on his hot cup of coffee.

"Do you know where Kiser could have gone when he took off the night before last?"

"I'm guessing he went to Judge Elliott's farm east of Humboldt. Kiser and the judge are tight and spend a lot of time together. It's a known fact that the judge also skipped town yesterday when he heard what you did at the saloon."

"We'll be paying him a visit soon, but right now, he's not a threat to anyone," said Sawyer. "We need to concentrate our time today at the land office, the saloon, and the judge's chambers. I looked around in there yesterday a little, although I'm almost positive that he took all his records with him."

"What about the bank files? Hopson is the one that should have the foreclosure papers for the land he stole from the farmers," said Craig.

"I've already talked to my sister Nancy Lou about that. She and the bank clerk will search for the records there. That is, if the clerk wants to keep his job and work for her."

"Sounds like a plan," said Craig. "I'll start carrying out Kiser's things from the cell if you want to clear his desk."

"Okay, but finish your coffee first."

Craig took one last drink, put his cup up, and started to work on cell one.

Sawyer sat at the desk and sipped his coffee, looking around the small office. After a few more sips, he pulled out the desk drawers and went through the contents. When he pulled the center drawer open, he spied a small book, inside of which were written several columns of dates and dollar amounts. He put it back in the drawer, intending to look it over later. Then, when he was finished and Craig had cleared the cell, the door opened and his sister Nancy walked in.

"You won't believe this," she said with her hands on her hips. "Someone broke into the bank last night and stole all the money. Willard, the clerk, said there was over three thousand dollars in the safe room when he left work the day of the shooting, and now it's gone."

"Are you kidding me?" asked Sawyer.

She took two steps toward his desk. "No. They broke in through the back door and took the money."

"What about all the bank records?" asked Sawyer.

"As far as Willard knows, they were not touched."

"Good. Come on, Craig, let's go to the bank and see if they left any clues."

"Sawyer," continued Nancy, "the bigger problem is what we're going to do about our depositors. All their money is gone, and I don't know what to do."

"Go to your barn and look in the feed bin. My bag is in there, and you'll find more than enough in it for the bank to continue operating."

"You have that much money?" asked his bewildered sister.

"Yes. You get the money while we investigate the robbery."

Sawyer and Craig made their way to the bank and tapped on the locked front door so the clerk would let them in.

"Come on to the back," said the clerk as he escorted the two lawmen through the bank.

"Nancy said your name is Willard, is that right?" asked Sawyer.

"Yes sir, and so you know, I never liked what went on here, but I needed a job to feed my family," said Willard.

Sawyer looked at the back door and then peered out into the alley. Something caught his eye, so he went down the two steps to examine the ground. He moved slowly, following a trail along the alleyway and stopping when he came to two piles of horse manure on the ground forty feet away behind a vacant building. Laying on the ground next to the building was a crow-bar. This clue led him to believe the two horses that had been tied at that location belonged to the thieves. He then followed their tracks south down the alley until it intersected with Elm Street. He circled the intersection and then walked back to the bank.

"The robbers used a crowbar to get the door open. It's lying against the back of that building where the horse droppings are located. That's where they had their horses tied while they robbed the bank. Only two men broke in through the back door. Then they mounted up and rode south to that street and turned east. You can tell by the hoofprints that the horses were in a full-out run once they got about a hundred yards from the alley."

Craig rubbed the stubble on his face. "Sheriff, you reckon Judge Elliott and Sheriff Kiser broke into the bank?"

Sawyer looked at the bank clerk. "Willard, are any of the bank's records missing, or is it just money?"

"Nothing is missing but the money, but we need to get it back soon. When the depositors find out we've been robbed and their money is gone, there could be hell to pay around here."

"That's being taken care of as we speak. I have enough money to cover the bank until we find the robbers." Sawyer turned back to Craig. "To answer your question, I don't think it was Kiser and Judge Elliott. If it had been them, I'm sure they would have stolen the bank's records, since the judge signed all the foreclosure papers. Do you mind checking around town at the mercantile store, blacksmith shop, and maybe the livery stable, and see if you can find out who that crowbar belongs to?"

"I can do that," said the deputy.

"Willard, keep the bank closed until Nancy gets back with my money, and then you can open up the front doors. You can even let people know that the bank was robbed last night, but make sure to tell them that their money is safe here at the bank."

"Sheriff, did you know that two strangers rode into town with Nathaniel and Howard on the stage two days ago?" said Willard. "I was at the stage office to meet Mr. Hopson when they came to town. I first thought that they might be more men associated with the banker, but I never saw them talk with Nathaniel or Howard. I'm wondering if they could be involved?"

"I had forgotten all about those two," said Craig. "I saw them going into the hotel and later walking around town after the shooting at the saloon."

"Were they wearing suits and bowler hats?" asked Sawyer.

"Yeah, they were," said Craig. "Did you see them too?"

"Yes, I got a glimpse of them at the saloon after the shooting,. I just figured they were townspeople," said Sawyer.

"I had never seen them before until that day," said Craig. "One of us should go to the hotel and see if they're still in town."

"I'll go to the hotel, while you try to find out where that crowbar came from," said Sawyer.

Chapter Four

Rufus and Avery rode east out of Humboldt after breaking into the bank and taking all the money they could find in the safe room. It was late, but Rufus wanted to put some miles between them and the town.

"Rufus, where're we going? It's mighty dark out here on horseback," said Avery.

"We'll find a good place to camp and hold up until daylight. That judge is supposed to have a farm out this way somewhere."

"What does the judge have to do with anything?" asked Avery.

"I have orders for us to kill Judge Elliott and Sheriff Kiser. We'll find a house and stay in it for the night."

"Are you saying that we find a house, kill whoever is in it, and spend the night?"

"It's that or we sleep on the ground without bedding or food. What would you rather do?"

"You know me. I ain't got a problem killing anyone, and if I get a choice between a nice bed and the ground, I'll take the bed."

"Good. Keep your eyes peeled for a farmhouse on that side of the road, and I'll watch this side," said Rufus.

A quarter of a mile farther south, they noticed the faint glow of a kerosene lantern through the underbrush and forest. It was swaying back and forth, like someone was walking outside.

"I bet there's a house in those trees and someone is going to the outhouse," said Avery.

"Hold up and let's talk about this before we do anything," said Rufus. "I'll give you a few minutes to ride in close and leave your horse. You get into position so you can kill whoever comes to the door. I'll ride in and get their attention, and when I say Humboldt, that will be your sign to kill. I'd prefer it if you use your knife, so you don't make a lot of noise."

"Are you ready for me to start up to the house?" asked Avery.

"Yeah, get goin'."

Rufus shook his head. His partner had to be the dumbest man he'd ever worked with. But at least Avery didn't mind doing the dirty work.

Rufus sat at the road for five minutes before he walked his horse up to the house and stopped about twenty feet from the door. "Hello, in the house. I'm lost and need directions to a farm out this way."

The door opened, and an elderly man sporting a goatee and wearing nothing but his long johns stood in the doorway holding a single-barreled shotgun. "Who are you, and what do you want this late at night?"

"I'm John Brown, and I'm trying to find Judge Elliott's farm."

The man motioned to the east with his hand. "The

judge has a farm three miles east and two south. Turn off this road just past the stream crossing the road."

"Much obliged. Can I give my horse a drink from your water trough? I rode him hard from Humboldt."

Avery came from around the corner of the house and shoved his knife between two of the old man's ribs, puncturing his heart. The man dropped the shotgun and tried to take hold of the wall, but his knees buckled, and he went to the ground gasping for air. Avery reached down, pulled the knife out, and pushed it back in. Blood began to seep out of the corners of the man's mouth. Avery pulled the knife from the dead man's body one last time and cleaned off both sides of the blade on the farmer's long johns. He went through the door, looking for his next victim, but the house was empty.

"You can come in now," Avery said from the doorway.

"Help me pull his body away from the front of the house. After that, we can see if there's anything to eat," said Rufus.

Once inside the house, Rufus cooked eggs and bacon before they turned in for the night.

After eating more of the dead man's food for breakfast the following morning, Rufus said, "We'll ride hard until we're close to the judge's house and play it the same way as we did here."

"But we don't know if I can sneak up on the judge like I did this old coot, and it'll be in broad daylight," said Avery.

"For once, you're right. We'll find his farm, then I'll decide what I want to do. Now, finish your coffee so we can get on the trail."

Chapter Five

Sawyer entered the hotel and tapped the bell on the counter. The desk clerk came into the lobby from the dining hall.

"Hello, Sheriff, what can I do for you?"

"What's your name, mister?"

"I'm Martin Platinum, but everyone calls me Marty."

"Nice to meet you. Are the two strangers that checked in two days ago still in their rooms?"

"I'm not sure. They paid for a whole week, although I haven't seen them since late yesterday. If you would like, I can go up to their rooms and see."

"Give me the room keys, and you stay where it's safe. I'll go alone in case of trouble."

"Yes, sir. I didn't consider there could be trouble. Here are the keys to rooms ten and twelve."

Sawyer took the stairs to the second floor and stood against the wall before reaching over and knocking on the door. No answer. He removed his gun from its holster, turned the knob, and shoved the door open, expecting gunfire. When nothing happened, he craned his neck to look into the room. It was empty. Two chairs were in front of the window like the men had been watching the street. Sawyer went to the other room, and it was also empty. He went back down to the lobby where he was met by Deputy Craig.

"I just talked to the telegraph operator, and he said that someone busted the lock on his front door last night."

"Did he say if the thieves stole anything?" asked Sawyer.

"No, he said that everything seemed to be where he'd left it except for the telegraph key. He thinks it was moved. I'm on my way to the livery stable to question Harry about selling two horses to those strangers yesterday. I told Mr. Hoffman that one of us would investigate the break-in later."

"How do you know they bought horses?"

"Lester Higgins saw one of them with ponies out behind the hotel after dark yesterday."

"Okay, you go to the livery, and I'll talk to the telegraph operator," said Sawyer. "Let's meet back up at the jail."

Sawyer went straight to the telegraph office. "Hello, Mr. Hoffman. Craig tells me you got broken into last night?"

"Yep, they broke the lock and splintered the door jamb. It looks like they may have kicked it in. You can't see any marks from a crowbar or other tool along the door and the frame."

"I saw that when I came in. Are you missing anything?"

"That's what's strange. I ain't missing one blasted thing, not even my petty cash."

Sawyer was in deep thought when the telegraph key started to tick. The operator got out his pencil and paper to decipher the Morse code. When he finished decoding what came over the wire, Sawyer asked, "Could someone come in here and send a telegram on their own if they knew how to operate the telegraph?"

"They could if they knew Morse code. But why would they break in to do that?"

"Maybe they didn't want anyone to know their business. If they sent a message on their own, would you be able to tell who they sent it to?" asked Sawyer.

"No, that would be impossible."

"How about sending a message and asking if any of the other telegraph offices received a communication from you last night after dark?"

"I don't know if that'll work. I've never done that before."

"You do that, and if you get a reply, please bring it to the sheriff's office."

Sawyer left the telegraph office and started back to his headquarters so he could document everything he had learned so far.

He was still sitting at his desk, jotting down the facts as he remembered them when Deputy Craig walked in the door.

"Have a seat and tell me what you found out," said Sawyer.

"Like I told you earlier, the town drunk, Lester, said he saw one of those men with two horses behind the hotel. I talked to Harry at the livery stable, and he sold two horses to one of those fellers. I showed him the crowbar you found, which also belongs to him."

"Based on what you and I've uncovered, I'm confident that the two strangers robbed the bank and then took off toward the east. I'll get my horse and see if I can pick up their trail. You stay in town and keep your eyes peeled for them in case they come back."

Craig opened the door to sit on the porch and watch the street. "Hey, Sawyer! Here comes Hoffman, and it looks like he's in a big hurry."

Sawyer walked outside and saw the telegraph operator waving a handful of papers in the air. "What do you have for me, Mr. Hoffman?"

"I would have never believed it, but I got a reply from the operator in Kansas City. He said I sent a message to Senator Bass last night, and the senator replied. Here's the message that was sent to the senator. And here's his reply."

Sawyer read the two telegrams before handing them to Deputy Craig. "Thanks, Mr. Hoffman, for bringing the messages to me. They're an important piece of our investigation."

"I'm just glad to be of service, and I hope you catch those two outlaws," said Mr. Hoffman as he turned and started up the street.

Sawyer touched Deputy Craig on the arm and motioned with his head for them to go back inside the office. "It appears that those two work for Senator Bass, and so did Hopson, McMillan, Judge Elliott, and Sheriff Kiser. If this don't beat all." Sawyer slammed his hand on the desk. "I was sure that the killing and stealing was over."

He kicked his chair, knocking it over. "I'm so upset

that a greedy US senator is behind all this. He had my folks murdered and their house burned to the ground over a few dollars. I gotta find the judge's farm before he and Kiser get killed. It would be nice to question them both, now that I know who is behind this whole criminal operation, and let them know that the senator had ordered them to be eliminated. They might want to turn state's evidence against the senator."

"I'm pretty sure Judge Elliott's farm is about six miles east and two south. I think a stream crosses the road close to the lane that goes to the house," said Deputy Craig.

"That's where I'm heading. If I'm not back by morning, I'm probably dead."

Chapter Six

Rufus and Avery left their horses tied in a line of trees that ran the

entire length of the creek that bordered Judge Elliott's property. The two killers had ridden east of the farm, but there wasn't a good location from which they could sneak up to the house. They had to backtrack and ride in the creek bed to avoid being seen.

Rufus whispered to Avery, "Get on your stomach and crawl through that cornfield to the house. When you're in position, wave at me, and I'll sneak around to the front. You come through the back door as soon as you hear me bust the front door in, and we'll catch him in a crossfire."

"But what if the back door is locked?" asked Avery.

"Are you that dumb? Kick the door in and come in ready to fill him with lead."

Rufus was still shaking his head in disgust, muttering cuss words as Avery crawled off toward the back of the house. Rufus waited in silence, and when he finally saw his partner wave his hand, he ran to the front of the house and used his shoulder to bust through the front door. Judge Elliott was taken by surprise but managed to get off one shot before he was hit with lead from the front and the back. He was dead by the time he hit the floor.

"You check the other rooms," said Rufus to Avery, who began to open doors.

"The house is empty. I better go check the barn," said Avery.

"I'll go with you."

Rufus went through the front of the barn while his partner came in through the back. He checked the tack room as Avery looked in the horse stalls. When Rufus came out of the tack room, he asked, "Did you see any sign of fresh horse crap in one of the stalls?"

"Yeah, that first one had quite a bit in it, like a horse was there for a few days."

"Okay. I'm going outside to try to find which way he left. You go get our horses and bring them back here."

Rufus began looking for tracks outside the barn doors and in the dirt lane. He followed what he thought could be the tracks of Sheriff Kiser all the way to the north–south road. He waved his hat in the air to get Avery's attention, and his partner brought the horses out to the lane.

"I'm not sure about tracks, but it looks to me like whoever left from the judge's house rode north. Look and see if you can determine what direction he went."

Avery dismounted. "I ain't very good at tracking, but I'll give it a go." He sauntered around the cross-roads, looking in each direction before he pointed north. "I think he went that way."

"That's what I thought too. Mount up. We'll ride north and see if we can find him."

They rode the two miles back to the main road that traveled east and west and stopped in the middle of the crossing. There, they began to move their horses in a circle while they studied the ground looking for tracks.

Avery finally spoke. "It probably wasn't a good idea to stop right here. We ain't did nothing but destroy Kiser's tracks."

Rufus was embarrassed by his mistake. He pointed east and said, "I think he went east. Let's ride."

They stopped at a farmhouse close to the road within the next hour. A man, woman, and three kids were planting turnips in the garden next to the road. "Howdy, folks," said Rufus. "We're hunting for a feller that came by earlier today. Did you happen to see him ride past?"

"Nope, we ain't seen no rider on the road today, and we been out here since sunup," said the man, wiping sweat from his brow.

Avery started to say something, but Rufus stopped him. "Thanks for your time. We'll be moseying on down the road. Come on, Avery, let's keep going."

Avery waited until they were farther down the road before he finally spoke. "Do you want me to go back there and kill that family so they can't tell anyone we came by?"

"No, they don't matter none. I'm fearful that we came the wrong way. We should have ridden west."

"I've been thinking about what I would do if I was in Kiser's place. I would probably ride south and go into the Indian Territory, where no one knew me," said Avery.

"Have you been thinking that and not sharing it with me as we rode out of the way for two hours? I swear, sometimes you really get me riled up something fierce. We wasted all this time, and you thought he would go into the Territory."

"Yep, that's what I would do," said Avery, nodding his head.

"Okay, let's head that way and see if we can catch up with him. Have you ever been in Indian Territory before?" asked Rufus.

"Nope, but I hear tell that it's nice. The only law is US marshals, and you never see them."

The farmer and his family waved at the two men when they rode by again. Neither Rufus nor Avery waved back.

Chapter Seven

Sawyer found the lane that would take him to Judge Elliott's house and contemplated whether to ride on in or dismount and walk in so he could stay hidden as much as possible. He finally decided to take a chance and see what would happen. Holding the reins in his left hand and his gun in his right, Sawyer walked his horse up to the house and dismounted. The front door was open, so he stayed clear of the opening in case the judge had a gun and was waiting on him. With his back to the outside wall, Sawyer peered cautiously into the front room and saw Judge Elliott lying dead on the floor in a pool of blood. Sawyer thought about going inside, but at the last moment, he went around to the back door to make sure he was alone and found it wide open as well. Someone had kicked it loose.

He took his time as he eased through the kitchen and then checked the rest of the rooms in the house. The front room was the last place he examined. The judge hadn't been dead long. His blood was still fresh and hadn't started to crust yet.

Sawyer took a second pass through the house, searching for evidence that might reveal who the old man worked for. From under the bed in what looked like Judge Elliott's bedroom, he pulled out a small bag, and inside it was cash money, a ledger book, and a few other papers. Sawyer took everything outside with him and hung the bag on his saddle horn.

He walked around in the front yard looking for tracks and then headed toward the barn, finding evidence that three horses had been there that morning. The horse's dung outside the barn was still soft and warm to the touch. It had to be the two strangers who had robbed the bank and killed the crooked judge. Inside the barn, he discovered a horse had been in one of the stalls, and it looked like it had also left this morning. Sawyer mounted up and rode down the lane until it intersected with the north–south road. He could tell by the tracks that horses had left the road to the judge's house, one horse going south, and the other two heading north.

He figured the lone set of tracks going south most likely belonged to Sheriff Kiser. The two sets going north were probably the two men he was after. Another thought came to mind. Maybe Sheriff Kiser had killed the judge before the two strangers got to him.

Either way, he had to go after all three men, and the odds were in favor of tracking down the two strangers more easily. With any luck, they would soon figure out that they were heading in the wrong direction and turn south. And he would be ready for them when that happened.

Sawyer rode north and turned east on the intersecting road, thinking the two men hadn't returned toward town yet, or he would have met them on the road. He'd been on the road a short distance when he saw two horses coming toward him. Slowly, he pulled his gun out of its holster and held it down by his leg until the two men were in gun range.

"I'm Sheriff McCade, and you two are under arrest for robbing the bank and for murder."

The man closest to him reached for his gun and was bringing it out of the holster when Sawyer fired and missed. Sawyer fired a second time as the man got his gun into play, about to fire back at him. The third shot from the sheriff's gun toppled the man off his horse.

The second rider spurred his horse and took off at a dead run down the road. He hunkered over the horse's neck, and Sawyer fired three more times—only to miss all three shots. He wheeled his horse around to go after the assailant but then thought better. His gun was empty and needed reloading, and there was no way he could refill the spent cylinders while riding at full speed.

The sheriff dismounted and reloaded his Colt Dragoon, looking down the road and watching the rider vanish out of sight. At least he had killed one of the outlaws. The dead man's horse stood close to the corpse. Sawyer bent down, put his arms around the man's chest, and lifted with all his might. It was an immense struggle since the man easily weighed over one hundred and fifty pounds. Sawyer eventually had to put a rope around the corpse's chest to secure its arms so he could lift it. He finally got the body laid across the saddle on its stomach with the legs and arms dangling. Sawyer tied it securely before their short journey back to Humboldt.

He would need his other guns, and maybe a pack-horse loaded with supplies to take with him to track down the other outlaw, and then there was still Sheriff Kiser to bring in. Was Sawyer expected to go after both the robber and the ex-sheriff? The two robbers were now also murderers. They had killed Judge Elliott, even though he had deserved to die because he'd signed off on all the deeds that Hopson stole from good, hard-working folks.

The judge deserved a decent burial even though he was a crook. Sawyer would send the undertaker to collect the judge when he was back in town.

As he was passing a path to a small farmhouse, he heard a cry for help as a girl of about fourteen ran toward him on the trail. He stopped and waited. "My grandpa is dead at the house! I think someone shot him. He's covered in blood and lying in the weeds."

"Okay, I'll take a look. You wait here."

Upon a thorough examination, Sawyer determined that the man had been stabbed with a knife, most likely the day before, since rigor mortis had already set in. Sawyer went into the house to look around. Two beds had been slept in, and two people had eaten breakfast in the kitchen. That was all he needed to see to pin this man's murder on the two men he was going after.

"You run on home, and I'll send the undertaker out here to collect the corpse," said Sawyer as he rode back to where the girl waited for him on the road.

"But sir, I don't think my ma and pa can afford the undertaker. We're poor folks and barely make ends meet," said the child through her sobs.

"It's all right. I'll see that he gets a proper burial.

You tell your folks to come into town later to see when the service will be."

"Thank you, Sheriff," said the girl before she started walking across the field. Sawyer went back into the house, pulled a quilt off the bed, and used it to cover the corpse until the undertaker could get out there.

Chapter Eight

Rufus looked over his shoulder every few minutes to see if the sheriff was on his tail. The little skirmish on the road had been a close call. Avery hadn't been as lucky and had gotten himself killed, but the dead man's loss was his gain. The sheriff had spent his time shooting it out with Avery while he got away.

All he knew about Indian Territory was that it lay to the south, and that was where he needed to go to find Sheriff Kiser and get away from Humboldt.

He had been running his horse for the past five miles, and the animal was beginning to slow down and tire out, in need of water and rest.

A man and woman in a wagon were coming his way. He stopped his horse beside the road, and when the wagon was close enough, he raised his hand and said, "Excuse me, but could you tell me if I'm on the right road to Indian Territory?"

"Yep, you remain on this road, and it'll take you to the trading post on the river. When you leave the post, you continue south to the Territory," said the man.

Rufus nodded at the man and started on down the road, letting his horse walk for a little while to give it rest. He kept watch behind him for the sheriff but never saw anyone. It would be time to eat soon, and he hoped that the trading post would have some cooked food. If Sheriff Kiser had come this way, Rufus figured he could catch up to him by tomorrow.

Another two miles down the trail, he came to a Y in the road. Both branches were going in a southern direction, but he needed to figure out which to take. He wanted to avoid making the same mistake he'd committed when they left the judge's property. He dismounted and walked a few yards down each road until he saw some loose soil had been torn up by a horse's hooves. He mounted back up and followed the tracks of the running horse at a fast pace. The tired animal had been ridden hard and when they came to a branch that crossed the road, Rufus dismounted and led his horse to the water's edge before getting on his stomach and drinking his fill of water. His horse was still sucking up water when Rufus pulled on the reins and made him step away from the creek long enough to mount.

He was beginning to get hungry since it was after his noon mealtime, and the eggs he'd had for breakfast were long gone. He hoped this road would take him to the trading post that the man had told him about.

Chapter Nine

Sawyer rode into Humboldt leading the horse with the dead man lying across the saddle. People stopped on the boardwalk and in the street to watch their new sheriff bring a corpse into town. Sawyer nodded at some and tipped his hat at a few more as he made his way down the dusty street to the undertaker's office. He tied both horses to the hitch rail and was in the process of unloading the corpse when the undertaker and his hired hand came out to assist.

"This is one of the men that robbed the bank. There are two more dead bodies I would like you to collect," said Sawyer.

"Let's get this one inside, and you can give me directions to the other two and how you intend for me to get paid," said the undertaker.

The three men lifted the corpse off the horse and carried it into the back room of the parlor. Sawyer went through the man's pockets and recovered what money he found.

He counted out forty dollars and handed it to the

undertaker. "This should cover the burial of the three men. One is Judge Elliott, and I don't know who the other man is. But I talked to his granddaughter, and his family are supposed to come into town later today to see when the burial can take place."

"This will be sufficient for three men. I know where Judge Elliott lives, and you can direct Allen to the other man. He knows this area well."

Sawyer gave the man directions and went back outside. A small crowd had gathered to find out who the dead man was. After a short explanation to the group, he led both horses to the livery stable. The hustler took the reins of Sawyer's horse. "Do you want me to unsaddle him and give him a helping of grain?" asked the hustler.

"Yeah, although I may need him in an hour or so."

Sawyer looked in the dead man's saddlebags and found no evidence or anything of value. However, inside the satchel tied to the saddle was a bag of money and papers. He removed that bag and then the one from his horse that he had found at Judge Elliott's house and took them back to the jail.

Deputy Martin was coming down the boardwalk about a block ahead of him, so Sawyer went into the sheriff's office. When the deputy came through the door, Sawyer looked in the satchel he had taken off the dead man's horse.

"I hear you brought one of the robbers in to the undertaker."

"Yeah, but the other one got away and headed south toward Indian Territory. I'm going to see what's in this bag and then decide what to do next. They killed an old man between here and Judge Elliott's place. The judge is dead, and it looks like Kiser had been staying there but escaped and headed south. I suspect the two robbers killed the judge and were trying to go after Kiser when I ran into them. I killed one, but the other took off in the same direction as Kiser, and I couldn't go after him with an empty gun."

"You realize you can't chase them into Indian Territory, don't you?" asked Craig. "That's under federal jurisdiction."

"I know. I wouldn't consider doing it at all, but that other feller is a murderer, and I can't for the life of me let him just ride off. What if he decides not to go into the Territory and goes somewhere else?"

"What do you want me to do?" asked Craig.

"I want you to stay here in town. I'm going to ride south to the two trading post that are located between here and the territories, and see if the men have come by there. I'm acquainted with each of the couples who operate them, and hopefully, I can get there before the killer."

"Okay, be careful. I'll watch the town in case he comes back. I'm sorry, but I don't know what the man looks like. I just know he's a stranger and not a local."

"That's quite all right. Unfortunately, things were happening so fast that I didn't get a good look at his face. I know he wears a bowler hat and had on a brown striped shirt, but that's not much to go on, especially if he decides to change clothes."

Sawyer picked up the satchel from the judge's house and the money sack off the desk. "I'm going to take this to the bank and then be on my way. I'll be back in a day or two."

There were no customers in the bank when he

entered the lobby. He nodded to the clerk and knocked on Nancy Lou's office door before opening it.

"Hello, sister. I brought you a little money I took off one of the robbers. It's not much, but it's a start. I also have a bag I found at the judge's house that I want to keep safe. You can take the money and deposit it in the bank, and then could you lock the bag up, so no one goes through it?"

"Thanks to you, we have more than enough funds to operate the bank. I've been going through all the fore-closure papers and found the deeds to the farms stolen by the crooks. I'll set up a meeting with the victims and let them know our plans to give them back their property."

"That's good. I know those poor folks will appreciate that. You may want to have Deputy Craig notify the heirs of the ones who were murdered."

"That's a good idea. I'll do that once I figure out who they are. What are you up to, since you brought in one of the robbers?"

"I'm riding south to see if I can catch up with Kiser or the man that killed the judge. I have evidence that he's also been ordered to kill Kiser, to keep him from talking. But I won't pursue the killer into Indian Terri-tory, even though he murdered an old man on the road to Judge Elliott's house. Anyway, I'll be back in a couple of days, and we can talk more."

"I wish you wouldn't go, but I know you must do your job."

"I know. I have to. I'll see you in a few days."

He gave his sister a hug and left the bank.

Sawyer went to Adams Mercantile and bought himself a bedroll and ground tarp, plus a small coffee pot and cast-iron skillet. He purchased enough provisions to last two days, then headed to the livery stable after his horse.

He waited while the hustler saddled the pony and brought him to the barn door. "He's been fed and watered, so he should be good to go until dark," said the man.

"Thanks."

Sawyer knew the way to the trading post north of the Neosho River since he had bought a packhorse and supplies there a month ago. He pushed his horse to cover the miles, which were easy to travel since the terrain was open.

He slowed down when he was a half mile from the trading post and veered off the road so he could come in from the west. The corral and back of the building faced the west, so he could see if any horses were in the horse pen or tied up behind the building. There was nothing in the rear of the building and no horses in the pen, so he rode on around to the front of the store and dismounted.

A good scout looked at everything around him, and this situation was no exception. He scoured the ground for horse tracks and fresh dung, noting that at least two separate horses had been there today. He also noticed two distinct types of boot prints leading to the store from where the horses had been.

Sawyer stepped through the open doorway with his hand on the butt of his gun handle in case trouble awaited him.

"Howdy, young man. Do you need another packhorse this trip?" asked the shopkeeper, recognizing him from before.

"No, not this trip. I'd like something to eat and information about a couple of travelers that were here earlier today."

"I have venison stew and cornbread. Let me get that, and then we can talk about the two men."

Sawyer held off asking questions until he was finished eating. The stew hit the spot, and when he was done, he sat back to talk to the shopkeeper. "Did Sheriff Kiser stop by here earlier today?"

"Yep, he came in and bought enough provisions to last most men three or four days. He said he was heading into the Indian Territories to the unassigned land, to take up ranching and maybe open a saloon."

"What do you mean by unassigned lands?" asked Sawyer.

"It's government land that ain't been given or assigned to Indians. No one owns the land, and I hear that army troops will run you off if they catch you homesteading it."

"About what time did Kiser leave here this morning?"

The man scratched his beard and squinted his eyes, trying to remember. "I reckon it was around nine, give or take an hour."

"Tell me about the other man."

"Now, he was a real doozy. He weren't from around these parts and was about as friendly as a bull buffalo. He came in demanding to know which way Sheriff Kiser went. When I told him I didn't know, he stuck a gun in my face and made me tell. All I could say was he rode south toward the river."

"Was the man wearing a brown striped shirt and a funny-looking hat?"

"Yep, that was him, all right. But, say, why are you after those two anyway?"

"I'm the new sheriff in Allen County, and Kiser is wanted for cheating people out of their land. The other man is wanted for bank robbery and murder."

"Well, I'll be doggone. I hope you catch both of those crooks. I suspect Sheriff Kiser will bed down someplace near Coffee's Trading Post. It's right before you get to the border. I'm not sure what that other feller might do. He didn't seem like the frontier type."

"Did you give the second man directions to Coffee's Trading Post?"

"Yep, but I told him to follow the road to the Neosho and then turn east until he comes to the bridge. He's going to make it there today by way of the bridge, but that way will cost him at least two or three hours of daylight."

Sawyer grinned at the man's remark. "Thanks for the food and the information." He laid two greenbacks on the counter and walked out.

Chapter Ten

Rufus was pleased that he'd gotten the man to give him the directions and information he'd needed. It always fascinated him that a gun in someone's face seemed to make them want to answer his questions. The man inside the trading post had been no different. He had finally told Rufus what he'd wanted to know, since the gunman had been ready to kill for it. Rufus wanted to get on with it and kill Kiser. He wasn't used to riding all day, and his thigh muscles and buttocks were already sore. That alone was enough to give him a bad attitude.

As he rode from the trading business, he noticed a trail going south. It looked recently used by a horse running or at least going faster than a walk. He stopped and looked back at the trading post and wondered if the man had given him some wrong directions after all.

Rufus urged his horse down the trail out of curiosity, and sure enough, the course grew broader, and he could still see where the soil had been disturbed by running horse hooves. The trail eventually intersected with another path that took him through tall timber, brush, and weeds. It was so hot riding through the forest with the trees blocking the wind that he began to sweat profusely.

After several miles of riding in the heat, his shirt was soaked, and so was his horse. His mouth and lips were parched, and he hadn't brought a canteen. How stupid he'd been to leave town, where he had all the comforts of modern civilization. He had grown up in Kansas City, and that was where he wanted to be, not on the back of some dumb horse chasing after a would-be dead man.

Suddenly his mount perked up and started to walk faster. Rufus pulled his pistol in case there was someone on the trail who had alerted his horse. It could be Indians since they were getting closer to Indian Territory. They went around a bend in the path and came across a swiftly flowing river.

What a sight for sore eyes. Rufus made the horse follow the trail to the water's edge and let it drink. He decided to stay in the saddle until the horse was finished since he had walked a couple of steps into the water, and Rufus didn't want to get his low-top shoes wet. While the horse drank, he began to pee, and it ran into the river. Rufus was disgusted by the idea of pee in the water. Now he'd have to go upstream to get himself a drink.

When man and animal had taken on water, Rufus looked across the river to the far bank and saw tracks going into the water where other horses had been cross-ing. Rufus had never ridden a horse across a river before, but how difficult could it be if others had been doing it?

Urged on by a couple of kicks, the horse stepped

forward until it started into the river. But it had different plans than Rufus did, and it stopped, not wanting to go any farther into the water. Rufus frantically kicked the horse's ribs, and the animal snorted and began to rear up and pitch. Not used to an upset horse, Rufus lost his grip and fell backward when the pony reared up a second time. He hit the ground with a thud, knocking the wind from his lungs.

Rufus lay on his back, trying to suck in air as the horse exited the water and started to eat grass. His rage took over, and he had to force himself to breathe normally again before getting up off the ground. Luckily, the horse's reins were still in his hand. Mad at the horse and himself, he tore a small limb off a sapling and mounted back up. He turned the horse toward the river and slapped it across its hindquarters with the switch until it ran into the water and went all the way under when it stepped into a deep hole in the river.

Rufus slid out of the saddle but held onto the bridle reins. The horse began to swim, and Rufus grabbed hold of the saddle, spitting water as he tried to stay afloat with the horse. It was only a short time until the horse's hooves touched the bottom of the river, and it could walk through the water again. Rufus could also feel the bottom of the river with his feet. He grabbed the reins to stop the horse so he could climb back into the saddle.

He was mad at himself for being so stupid and getting soaked. The horse had tried to warn him that there was a deep hole in their path, but he didn't pay attention to the animal's instincts. Now his hat was gone, and he would have to ride with wet britches and shoes.

When they were out of the water and safe on the south bank of the Neosho River, Rufus dismounted. He was leading his horse to some grass when he snagged his shirt on a locust thorn and ripped a gaping hole in the back. He wanted to lash out at someone or something, but it was just him and his horse.

After staking the horse so he couldn't wander off, he sat down and removed his shoes and socks. He walked back to the horse, took his bag from the saddle horn, emptied his bag, and hoped his spare clothes and money were still dry. They were. He stripped bare and changed into his spare shirt and pants but had to continue wearing his wet shoes. The wet clothes were useless to him, so he left them on the ground. He pulled his gun from the holster and started pushing damp powder and wadding out of the cylinders. Next, he cut a stick to move a dry piece of cloth through the cylinders to dry out any water. Fortunately, his powder flask was waterproof, and he could reload his weapon.

Darkness overcame the man-hunter, and he still hadn't reached Coffee's Trading Post. He had to decide whether to ride on in the dark or stop for the night without any provisions or bed clothing. He could ride on for a few miles and be on the watch for a homestead where he could spend the night. Yep, that's what he would do, and if anyone gave him any lip, he would kill whoever lived there.

An hour later, it was almost pitch dark since it was a new moon. He rode to the top of a small hill, and off to the east he could see a glow of light. That was where he would hole up for the night. Urging his horse to go faster, they covered the distance quickly. The glare he had seen was from a crude outdoor clay oven that an

Indian woman was using to make bread. She also had a fire built under a big pot in which she was cooking soup. This wasn't unusual though—many folks cooked outdoors so they didn't create extra heat in the house during the hot summer months.

He rode into the yard and called out. "Hello, I'm a weary traveler needing help."

The Indian that was cooking hurriedly went into the house and came back outside with a butcher knife in her hand. She didn't say anything. She just looked at the man on the horse. He thought it odd that she was silent, but then again, he hadn't been around many Indians before.

Rufus motioned to the fire where the pot was steaming. "I'm mighty hungry and could use a place to sleep for the night."

She nodded her head toward him, and from somewhere behind Rufus, a man spoke. "Do you have money to pay for the food and shelter?"

Rufus turned around to see a white man with a shotgun aimed at his head. "Now hold on, mister. I'm not here for trouble. I need food and a place to bed down. I have money to pay." He reached into his britches pocket, brought out three dollar bills, and showed them to the man.

The man lowered his gun. "Climb down and sit on that log over by the fire. The missus will spoon you a plate of food, and you can sleep back in the smokehouse."

Rufus did as he was told and watched the woman fill a plate of food for him. The man filled himself a plate and sat opposite Rufus, who ate what he'd been given, although it didn't taste all that good. As they ate, the woman went into the house and returned with some hides and a blanket.

"Where're you headed out this way in the dark?" the man asked in between smacking on his food.

"I'm going to Coffee's Trading Post. Do you know where that is?"

The man laughed and food spewed from his mouth. "Yep, it's two miles south of here. I reckon you could have already been there if you hadn't come here."

Rufus's face became red with rage at the man's laughter. But he decided to let it go and see if the man had seen Sheriff Kiser ride through.

"I'm looking for a man who came through this way earlier this morning. His name is Kiser. Did he happen to come by here?"

"Nope, not here, but he stopped at the trading post for supper and is most likely sleeping there tonight."

Rufus set his plate on the ground. "You saw him at the trading post today?"

"Are you deaf? I said he was at the trading post late this afternoon."

Rufus was getting madder as he sat there. "Would he be sleeping inside the building or outside somewhere?"

"I reckon he's most likely sleeping under the big oak tree on the west side of the building. They put out a couple of cots for travelers in the summer."

"How long will it take me to get there in the dark?"

"From here, I'd say half an hour."

"Do I just stay on the trail I was on back there?" asked Rufus as he pointed in the direction he had come from.

"Yep. Say, if you ain't goin' to eat the rest of that

food on your plate, pass it over here. We don't let food go to waste around these parts. Those skunks are too hard to skin to let the meat go to waste."

Rufus almost puked up his meal when he heard that he had been eating a skunk. The man laughed and said, "I was just funning you. It's not really a skunk, it's an opossum."

Rufus got up. "Thanks for the food." He handed the man a dollar. "I'm going to the trading post and catch up with my friend."

"You come back anytime, you hear?" the man said and laughed again.

Rufus mounted up and started back to the trail. He still felt like throwing up but thought better of it since he had no other food to fill his belly.

Chapter Eleven

Sawyer led his horse away from the trading post that was north of the Neosho River and followed the tracks of the horses that had been there earlier. He first noticed that one horse had run south on the trail. The second horse seemed to stand in the path, based on how the ground looked, and then it must have gone in the same direction as the first horse. The killer had seen Kiser's tracks and followed them instead of riding to the bridge.

Sawyer assumed the man had figured out that the directions he received from the store owner were wrong. Although it really didn't matter. He followed along on the men's trail, hoping he could get to Kiser before the killer did. He loped his horse as much as possible so he could get across the Neosho River before dark. Although the path went through and around timber, it was mostly level ground and easy to travel. Unfortunately, it was scorching hot, and he kept taking sips of water from his canteen for relief. Too bad his horse didn't have a place to get water, but it wouldn't be long before they came to the river.

The river should be easy to cross this time of year, Sawyer figured. It had been a while since they'd had rain, but he would still have to be careful not to guide his horse into a deep hole.

As he scanned the riverbank, he spotted where someone had started into the water, and the horse had acted up. Sawyer had crossed in this spot before, but this time he used a trail a few feet farther west. Once his horse started into the current, Sawyer kicked his feet free of the stirrups and held them high to keep his boots from filling with water. As they were coming up the south bank, he saw clothing remains scattered on the ground.

Sawyer camped where he was for the night. It would be dark soon, and he wanted to inspect the clothing that was left on the grassy earth. The britches were still damp, and the shirt had a rip in the back. He noticed something else on the ground and squatted down to pick up small patches of cloth that had been used as wadding for a weapon. The man had most likely fallen into the water and gotten soaked, then had to dry and reload his weapon. That would also explain the change of clothes. If only Sawyer knew what the man looked like, since he changed clothes and now would be unrecognizable. Unless he had kept his hat safe, it had probably fallen into the water and washed away.

Before Sawyer removed the saddle from his horse, he gathered wood for a small fire and laid out his bedroll. After a light supper of cold biscuits and bacon he purchased from Adam's store, he turned in for some shuteye. He wanted to be on the trail before daylight so he could try to make up time.

The breeze stopped during the night, and he woke up in the dark sweating from the humid air. With a stick, he rekindled his small fire and put water on to boil for coffee as he saddled his horse. By the new moon's position, he figured it must be about three in the morning. He would have to go slowly since there wasn't much light, but he decided to head out anyway. After two cups of coffee, he started down the dark trail. As soon as it was light he would urge his horse faster, but until then he was cautious—the last thing he wanted was to be slapped in the face by a limb or cause his horse to step in a gopher hole.

The morning sun began to rise in the east as he heard the faint sound of a single gunshot. Sawyer pulled back on the reins and listened. It had been so far away that he couldn't be sure what direction it had come from. He continued on, and in another quarter of a mile, it was light enough that he spotted where a horse had turned east. He stopped and thought for a few seconds, then turned east and followed. He could see the tracks better as the sun opened up the bright sky. Suddenly he rode up on a sod house, where an Indian woman was standing in front of a clay oven, cooking.

"Howdy, ma'am. I'm Sheriff Sawyer McCade, and I'm after the man that rode through here last night."

The woman said something in her native language, and a man came out of the house.

"He was here all right," said the man. "But he left when I told him that Coffee's Trading Post was only two miles away."

"What did the man look like, and what did his horse

look like? I know he changed his clothes at the river; I suspect he fell off his horse when they crossed."

"He had on a white and red checkered shirt and gray britches. That horse of his is a sorrel with two white stockings on its right side. I agree with you that he probably fell into the water. Come to think about it, his gear looked wet."

"So he rode on to Coffee's last night in the dark?"

"Yep, he lit out of here about two hours after sunset."

"Thanks," said Sawyer. He turned his horse around but then turned back to ask another question. "Did you shoot your gun a few minutes ago?"

"Nope, that wasn't me. It sounded like it came from the trading post."

"Much obliged," said Sawyer, and took off the way he had come.

If that shot had come from the post, he might be too late to save Kiser's miserable life, but he hoped he could get there in time to at least arrest the killer.

Chapter Twelve

Rufus rode slowly and stopped every few feet until he could make out the dark form of the trading post structure. He was about to proceed when he heard a horse nicker to the right of the building. He dismounted and tied his horse so it could graze while he crept forward on foot.

He eased toward the trading post slowly so he wouldn't make any noise and wake up Sheriff Kiser or the people inside. Once he was within fifty feet of the dark structure, he sat on the ground with his back against a tree and dozed off to sleep.

When he woke up, the sun was just beginning to rise on the horizon. The trading post was visible, as were several cots under an oak tree. He removed his gun and cocked the hammer, then sneaked up to the only cot that was occupied. Kiser's snoring could be heard before Rufus got close enough to shoot. If the man kept snoring, he could keep advancing on his prey.

Rufus stopped three feet from the sleeping ex-sheriff. After taking a deep breath, he aimed his gun, pulled the trigger, and watched as part of the man's head exploded. One shot was all it took.

Rufus ran back to his horse. It was time to get away before anyone saw him so he mounted, headed past the trading post, and kept going south until he was out of sight. A quarter mile away, he turned his horse off the road and headed west. If he rode a day's journey west and then turned north, he could ride another day or so and eventually get to Chisholm's Trading Post on the Arkansas River, a rough but well-known place where settlers traded with the Wichita Indians. Most cowboys called it Cowtown because of the incessant herds of cattle that came up the Chisholm Trail. But the locals called it Wichita because of the Wichita Indians who lived there. It was growing by leaps and bounds since the Atchison, Topeka, and Santa Fe Railways were all under construction in the area.

He needed to get to Cowtown to send his boss a telegram and find out what Senator Bass wanted him to do next. If he rode hard, he could make it in a couple of days, three at the most. But with no supplies, he would have to stop along the way and see if he could buy food or at least get directions to someplace where he could purchase provisions. It was stupid of him to have left with nothing for the road, especially not even a canteen or bedroll.

Riding cross-country for a few miles slowed him down; there were many gullies to cross and it was always slow going through timberland. Early in the afternoon he rode up on a farmhouse. Rufus stopped his horse far enough away in some trees and watched the homestead to see if anyone was home. Then, with his pistol in his hand, he advanced into the yard. When no one came outside to see who was there, he dismounted and knocked on the door. No answer.

Rufus was still holding his gun when he grasped the door latch with his other hand, and pushed the door open. He didn't see anyone as he walked inside and looked around. The coffee pot on the hearth was slightly warm, so whoever lived there must have gone to the fields to work. He searched the area they used as a kitchen and found flatbread and leftover salt pork.

He stole a canteen and two blankets, which he rolled up and tied to the back of his saddle. The well was nearby, so he watered his horse and filled the canteen before riding out from the property. From there, it was only a short distance until he saw a road angling northwest.

Rufus continued to ride northwest the rest of the day and camped that night on the banks of the Verdigris River. Since he had no food or coffee, he dry-camped without a fire.

The following morning, he was on the trail by daylight and had already ridden a few miles when he came to a tiny place called Coyville. It was all of three small houses and a store. He stocked up on supplies at the store and bought some bread and sliced beef meat. By talking with the locals, he learned that he could be in Eureka, Kansas, by nightfall if he pushed his horse.

Rufus noticed that the closer he got to Eureka, the more cattle he saw and the less farming. The town itself was primarily tiny log houses scattered along the road. There was a store, a blacksmith, a livery stable, a women's dress shop, and a few other businesses along the dirt street. At the livery stable, the owner got up from a wooden chair to greet Rufus as he dismounted.

"Howdy stranger, you want me to feed and water your horse?"

"I do, and if you know where a weary traveler could get a strong drink, I could sure use one."

"Sorry, we ain't got a watering hole yet, but you can get some supper down the street where those two horses stand in front of that house right there." The man pointed down the street.

Rufus walked to the house, had supper, and arranged to sleep in the folks' spare bed. Once he finished eating and had one last cup of coffee, he asked the man whose wife ran the place if there was somewhere he could get something to drink.

The man looked around to make sure his wife was out of hearing. "Down the street is a long, skinny log building with harness and tack for sale. Old Harold most likely has some shine you can buy."

"Thanks," said Rufus. "I'll be back later."

Chapter Thirteen

As he rode into the yard of Coffee's Trading Post, the first thing he saw was the man and woman who owned the place bustling around a stand of oak trees to the west of the store.

"Get on down from your horse. We had some misfortune here a little while ago," said the man.

Sawyer knew what it was before he walked to the cot and looked down at the late Sheriff Kiser. "I heard the shot. Did either of you see who did the shooting?"

The man and woman both shook their heads no. "We were still asleep when it happened, but I saw a man ride off to the south at a dead run when I got to the door. I can't tell you what he looked like since it was still dark, and I don't see too well."

Sawyer thought that was unfortunate, but figured he could track the man anyway. He looked down at the dead body again and went through Kiser's pockets. "This is the ex-sheriff from Humboldt over in Allen County. His last name is Kiser, and I was after him for cheating farmers out of their land. I'll search his belongings and see if he has any evidence like papers or deeds on him before we dispose of the body." He looked at the man and woman. "What's y'all's names, anyway?"

"We're Keith and Molly McDougal," said the man. "We should probably bury this feller before he stinks up the place and runs off business. I'm going to go to the shed and grab a couple of shovels."

"That's a good idea," agreed Sawyer. "I'll finish up here and help you with digging a grave."

It took the two men an hour to get a hole deep enough to put Kiser in and another thirty minutes to get the grave covered with dirt and tree limbs so wild animals couldn't dig him up.

Molly came outside with a water bucket and dipper when the men finished. "Here's some cool water from the well. I have ham cooking, and when you're ready, I'll fry up some eggs."

"Thank you, Molly," Sawyer said, and proceeded to drink two dippers of water before passing the dipper to Keith. "If you have enough eggs, I think I can eat a half dozen myself, and I'll pay you for the food."

Molly smiled. "I've got plenty. I'll make extra ham and biscuits so you can take some on the road when you leave here."

The three ate a big hearty meal, and Molly sacked up some food for Sawyer. He paid for his grub and headed out to pick up the trail of the shooter, which was harder to find now, since grass covered the course and he could see only a little dirt. It was slow going for a couple of miles, and eventually, the trail grew even harder to see. His army training as a scout had taught him to follow whole troops of soldiers, which was much easier than trailing one man on a horse. Troop movement meant there would be lots of tracks, and even some wagon or artillery ruts. He used to look for bloody bandages or other discarded waste, but now he was looking for the littlest thing, like a broken blade of grass or a trampled swath of undergrowth where horse's hooves had made marks.

Which was what he finally saw, an hour after setting out. The grass was bent over where the rider had turned west, and it wasn't much farther until Sawyer could tell the man had been running his horse by the way the ground was indented.

Soon, Sawyer would have to make some decisions about what to do. Would he continue on and spend days or even a week tracking the killer down, even though he didn't know what the man looked like or even his name? This man could hole up anywhere, and finding him could be almost impossible.

Sawyer urged his horse on and continued following the tracks west until he saw where the man had turned in a northwest direction. That would likely mean the killer was heading somewhere he was familiar with. Where was the man going, and what was his reason for going there? After thinking about it for a few seconds, Sawyer surmised that if it was him, he would go to the nearest telegraph office, update his boss, and wait for instructions.

Sawyer turned his horse northwest and took off on the same trail the killer had taken. If luck was on his side, he might catch up with him in the next town. Following the killer all over the state wasn't an option. If he didn't catch up to him in the next town, then he would turn back and return to Humboldt.

Sawyer followed the killer's trail across the countryside until he spied a farmhouse in the distance. He stopped long enough to survey the yard and the adjacent area, which was surrounded by tall trees. Within twenty-five yards of the house, a man wearing bib overalls stepped out with a shotgun, aimed it at Sawyer, and fired from the hip. Sawyer tried to shove himself from the saddle but wasn't fast enough. The lead pellets hit him on his left arm and the left side of his ribs and neck, resulting in a terrible sting.

He hit the ground and all the air left his lungs. After that, he could only think about trying to breathe and pulling his gun to protect himself.

The farmer and his wife came out to where he lay, and the man had the gun trained on Sawyer as he lay gasping.

"Wilber, you imbecile. You done shot a lawman," said the woman.

"What? I didn't see a badge. Help me get him up so he can catch his breath."

The man and woman sat Sawyer up, and he was able to breathe better. "Why did you shoot me?" he asked.

"Someone broke into our house this morning, and I thought you was them, returning to get more of our stuff."

"Sheriff, my name is Ruth. Let me look at your wounds." The woman took the end of her apron and wiped the blood away where the shot had entered in various places on his arm, examining the extent of his wounds.

Sawyer looked at the man while Ruth checked his ribs, arm, and neck for injuries from the birdshot.

"When was your house broken into, and what did he take?"

"The scoundrel came here while we were working in the field. He took some blankets, my canteen, and I don't know what else. I haven't had time to really look."

"I'm Sheriff Sawyer McCade from Humboldt. I'm tracking a murderer and need any information you can give me. What's your name?"

"Sorry, I'm Wilber. Let me help you up so we can go over by that tree, and Ruth can start plucking that birdshot out of you."

Sawyer got up, and the man held onto his arm as they walked to a massive oak tree with chairs and a bench situated in the shade. He was still a little dazed from the shot and the fall. Wilber sat him down in a wooden chair. "I'm mighty sorry that I shot you. I just assumed you were the same person who was here earlier."

"Next time someone comes into your yard, you may want to ask who they are before you shoot," said Sawyer.

Ruth washed blood from a few places on his cheek that had been hit, and used a slender knife with a sharp point to pluck the lead shot from his skin. At least all the lead was under the surface of the outer skin, so Sawyer wouldn't suffer any long-lasting injury. She spent about thirty minutes tending to his injuries. It was painful, but he gritted his teeth and let her doctor him.

"I've got all the shots I can find removed from your skin. I'm going after the whiskey jar, and I'll put a little on your wounds to stop infection. You can get by without bandages since most of the bleeding has stopped."

"Thanks," said Sawyer, although he was still mad that they had shot him.

Ruth returned with Wilber and poured whiskey on a cloth. She tapped the fabric on each wound, and the whiskey stung his raw skin, causing him to jump and make a face each time she applied it.

"Sheriff, the blankets and canteen are the only things missing. I reckon he needed something to sleep on," said Wilber.

"I reckon so. What's the nearest town northwest of here where a man could send a telegram?"

"I don't rightly know. We only get away and go into town about once a month, and I have no need to send telegrams, so I can't help you with that. The next little town northwest of here will be Coyville, but there ain't much there."

Chapter Fourteen

There were no boardwalks in Eureka, only dirt streets used by wagons, riders, and people on foot. Rufus walked around small mud puddles and passed an elderly couple on his way to the long, skinny building where he hoped to get a drink. He could see a lantern glowing inside, so he opened the door and went on in. A man came out from a back room of the building, drying his hands on a soiled apron.

"Howdy, I'm Harold, the owner of this place. What can I do for you, friend?"

"The gentleman at the boarding house told me that you might have some shine for sale."

Harold wiped his mouth with his hand before he said anything. "I might have a taste or two in my private room, if you want to follow me back there."

Rufus tagged along behind the man to a workroom that looked like it also served as a kitchen and bedroom. Sitting at a large rectangular table were two other men. A fruit jar of clear liquid and three glasses sat on the tabletop in front of them.

"Have a seat, and I'll get you a glass. It'll be ten cents a shot. This is Sam, and that feller is James. What would your name be?"

"I'm Dan Jones, and I'm just passing through."

Sam pulled out a deck of cards. "If you got any money, we can have a friendly poker game."

Rufus reached into his pocket and retrieved a roll of greenbacks, and the men began to play. After an hour of drinking the stout liquor and losing a fair amount of money, he was flat drunk. The whiskey was affecting his speech, and he couldn't focus on what he was doing. "I've had enough. It's time for me to leave," he slurred.

He stood on shaky legs and started to the front door, weaving and hitting the walls. Sam took him by one arm while James took hold of the other.

"Let us help you back to the boarding house so you don't pass out somewhere," said Sam.

Next thing he knew, Rufus woke up lying on the ground next to the leather shop. Something wet touched his face and caused him to open his eyes. He looked up into the face of the ugliest dog he had ever seen. "Get out of here, you mangy mutt!" As he wiped the dog saliva off his face, the pain in his head reminded him of the drinking he'd done the night before. The pain was at the back of his head, and when he ran his fingers through his hair, he felt a goose egg on the back of his skull.

Rufus held the back of his head and neck with one hand and used the other to assist himself with sitting upright against the building. Cobwebs were still fogging his vision as he tried to remember what had happened. His holster and money were gone. He got fighting mad at himself and at the two men. He recalled them offering to help him walk to the boarding house, but that was all.

He had to get up and go to the livery stable where he had left his clothing bag and the money he and Avery had taken from the bank. If that was gone, he would surely be a dead man. His boss detested anyone that stole or lost his money.

He slowly got to his fee, using the wall to hold on to, and started walking toward the street, since the livery stable was across the road. Unfortunately, the trek across the dirt street seemed to take forever. His first stop at the stables was the water trough, where he dunked his head into the water.

Even though he still had pain in the back of his head, the water helped to wake him up. He continued into the barn where the man running the place was forking hay to the only two horses in the stalls.

"You don't look so good today, stranger. What happened to you?" asked the hustler.

"It's none of your darn business. Where's my gear? I need to get something."

"It's right over in the corner where I left it."

It was a challenge for Rufus to bend over. The throbbing in his head was extreme, so he went down on his knees to look inside the bag. Sure enough, the money was still there, so he pulled out a few bills and put them in his shirt pocket.

"Saddle up my horse. I'm leaving town. Is there someplace where I can buy a gun?"

"Gould City is the most likely place for that. Did you lose yours last night?"

"That's none of your business either. How far is it to Gould City, and how do I get there?"

"You keep going west, and you'll find it later today."

Rufus had difficulty getting in the saddle but finally made it. He'd pay Harold a visit before he left town, and hopefully, those two who robbed him would be there. He walked his horse up the street, dismounted farther up the road, and returned to Harold's building on foot. The pounding in his head made it hard to maintain his balance, and he had to keep putting his hand on the side of buildings and on porch posts for support. When he got to the door of Harold's business, he opened it, entered, and closed it again without making a sound. He looked around for something he could use as a weapon and saw axe handles for sale. With a wooden shaft gripped tightly in his hand, he proceeded to the back room to find Harold in his bed snoring up a storm.

He poked the man in his ribs with the axe handle. Harold's eyes jerked open and he sat up, wiping his eyes. "What in tarnation are you doing here this early? I don't open for another hour."

Rufus poked him with the axe handle again. "Where are those two men that were drinking shine here last night?"

"I don't know. Sam said they were just passing by and wanted to drink."

"You're telling me they just happened to find their way in here, and you ain't never seen them before?"

"Yep, last night was the first time they've been here. Why are you looking for them?"

"They robbed me, and I aim to get my belongings back, so where are they?"

"I told you I don't know. Now get out of here and leave me alone."

Rufus swung the axe handle and it connected with the side of Harold's head, knocking him out cold. He went through the man's things and found an old navy pistol and holster. He put it on and continued searching until he found a powder flask, lead balls, and primer.

He walked out of the shop and mounted up, heading west. His next stop would be Gould, Kansas.

Chapter Fifteen

Sawyer's wounds were itchy and sore. He had an upset stomach and headache from falling off his horse and figured it was due to having a slight concussion. He still couldn't believe that Wilber had shot him. He would definitely be more careful in the future.

He felt like he was on a wild goose chase, but thought it best to see if the man he was after was in Coyville. Maybe he'd checked into a hotel while waiting on instructions from his boss. The people of Allen County had elected him sheriff, and with that came the responsibility to catch the killer and bring him to justice. He also had to determine what he would do about Senator Bass in Kansas City. That could be a challenging project since the senator was a powerful politician.

Coyville was much smaller than he expected. He rode down the single street and stopped at the only business in town, Coy's Store.

A clerk entered the shop from a doorway at the

back of the room. "Welcome to Coyville. What can I do for you, sheriff?"

"I'm looking for a man on a sorrel with two white stockings on the right side. He may have stopped in here for some supplies. Have you seen him in town?"

"Yep, he came through but has already gone. I'm sure he went on to Eureka when he left out of here this morning."

"I take it that there's no telegraph office in town?"

"That's right, the nearest one is in Cowtown. You might make it there in a few days if you ride hard."

"Thanks," said Sawyer, and went outside and mounted up. There was no use in continuing. It was time to return to Humboldt, where he had a duty to protect the townspeople. If he left now, he could camp on the Fall River and make it home by the following night.

He rode as the crow flew through the forest and fields. Raising cattle seemed to be the desired way for people to make a living in these parts. He thought about his friends in Texas and wondered how they were doing, gathering wild longhorns from the mesquite thickets. He had planned to be a part of the gathering but had to come home to kill the men who murdered his family and his sister's husband. He also thought about the waitress he had met in the café in Clarksville, Texas. She was the prettiest woman he had ever seen, and it had felt like love at first sight. Her name was Abigail, and when she'd kissed him in front of her house, he'd gone weak in the knees. There wasn't much he could do while on the trail of a killer, but when he got back to Humboldt, he would talk to Nancy about her and ask for advice about contacting her.

He'd been so lost in his thoughts he'd failed to realize he'd ridden right up to a river. The Fall River made for an excellent place to bed for the night and rest his tired, sore body. He set up camp before dark and had just finished his meal when two men rode up to the edge of his campsite. One called out, "Hello, in the camp. There're two of us. Can we ride in?"

"Come on in, but make sure those hands are empty when you do," replied Sawyer. He pulled out his guns and waited for his company to show themselves.

Two rough-looking young men rode in. They were in need of haircuts and beard trimming, and their clothes were filthy. They looked like a couple of riders who had been living in the wilderness for a while.

"If you have cups, I have plenty of coffee," said Sawyer.

"Much obliged. I'm Ezra Wilks, and this is my brother Joe Wilks. We're on our way to Wichita to kill a man."

Sawyer raised an eyebrow. "To kill a man? You don't say. I've never been to Wichita, but I know most folks call it Cowtown around here. I suppose you saw the badge on my shirt, and you're telling me you're going to kill someone?"

"We saw the badge, and that's why we asked to share your camp. We don't want trouble, and we don't want to cause any. We just want someplace to rest for the night where we don't have to sleep with one eye open waiting to get our throats cut."

"You're safe with me. I'm Sheriff Sawyer McCade from over in Allen County. That's northeast of here. I've been chasing a killer myself, but I'm turning back to go home. Sometimes, chasing an outlaw is like playing cards. You need to fold, leave the table, and pick up the game again later."

Ezra poured himself a cup and then handed the pot to Joe. "We ain't folding this time. The man we're after is named Walter Hicks. He and three other men broke into our homes on the Canadian River, north of the Chickasaw Nation. We'd cleared a plot of land, built two houses with our own hands, and married a couple of Chickasaw girls. We'd started raising families. One day, about three weeks ago, all that was taken from us." He had to stop talking and collect himself before going on.

"Joe and I had gone off hunting deer and turkey for the winter so we would have meat, and when we got back, our women and kids were all dead. We buried them and followed the tracks the killers left. We caught up with them at a settlement about thirty miles north of our homes, and that's when we learned who they were and what they looked like. We split up to watch the saloon, and I took the front, and Joe went around to the back. You tell him the rest, Joe."

"I saw one of the men exit the back door and go to the outhouse. That's when I decided to have a talk with him. He was sitting on the hole when I jerked the door open and put my knife to his throat. He told me that his name was Tommy, and Walter Hicks was the boss. The two men with them were Dillan Standifer and Joey Lester. Then I sliced him open right there on the hole and watched him bleed out like he had watched our families die."

"Now it's the remaining three you're hunting down?" Sawyer asked.

"No, there's only Walter left. We killed the other

two in the saloon that night, but we couldn't find Walter. He had gone home with a saloon girl, and we didn't see him leave."

"It seems like you fellers are off course if you're following him to Cowtown," said Sawyer. "Cowtown is northwest of here quite a-ways. I've been told it's another two days' ride."

"Walter tricked us on the trail back in the Territory. He had some people tell us he went to Coffeyville, and that's where we headed off. We wasted three days before we figured out he'd shaken us off his trail. We had to backtrack, and the best we can tell, that's where he is."

"Well, I wish you luck with finding this Walter feller. Have all the coffee you want. I'm turning in so I can get an early start tomorrow," said Sawyer, who went to his bedroll and lay down. To be safe, he pulled a blanket over himself and kept the .36 caliber Navy Colt in his hand under the blanket. His army days had taught him to always sleep armed.

Chapter Sixteen

Rufus rode into Gould City, Kansas, just after dark. The town was nothing more than a trading post and a few houses. He stopped at the store and went inside.

"Welcome, stranger. What can I do for you tonight?" asked a man who sat in a rocking chair at the end of the counter. He wore bib overalls and drank moonshine from a jar.

"You have any food a weary traveler could eat this late at night?"

"I sure do." The man turned his head toward a door in the back of the shop. "Wilma, throw some venison backstrap in the skillet for a customer." He smiled at Rufus. "My wife will fry you up some fresh venison tenderloin and taters for four bits. I've got some strong shine if you have a hankering for a taste." The man handed the jar to Rufus.

Rufus took a sip and wiped the back of his hand across his mouth. "Man, that's some strong liquor. I think I'll pass on it right now. Maybe I'll have another swallow before I leave. I'd also like to upgrade my gun if you have any I like."

"I've got a couple for sale. Come with me to the counter, and I'll show you what I have." He pulled out two guns from a shelf under the countertop. One was an older Colt, and the other was a Navy Colt like the one Rufus had, only newer. He looked at the Navy Colt and then pulled his from its holster. "How much boot do you want if I trade you this one for that Navy Colt you have?"

The man took hold of Rufus's gun, looked it over, and said, "I'll trade you for this gun and the meal for eleven dollars."

Rufus stood still for a few seconds and then stuck out his hand. "We have a deal."

He had finished loading the pistol when a woman came out from the back room carrying a plate of hot food. She set it on a small dining table against the north wall, close to a barrel of apples.

"Thank you, ma'am, it sure looks tasty."

When he finished his meal and paid his bill, he rode off, hoping he could locate a place to make camp and bed down for the night.

About a half mile from Gould City, he smelled smoke and stopped his horse, trying to figure out if someone had a campfire nearby. He rode a little farther and saw a faint glow through the trees, so he turned off the road and rode toward where he glimpsed the fire. When he was within hearing distance, he called out, "Hello, in the camp, can I ride in?"

"Come on in, but be aware that I have a gun trained on you if you try anything," said a man's voice.

Rufus sat still for a few seconds, deciding if he

wanted to ride in or not. Then he called out, "Don't shoot. My hands are empty."

There was no one visible in the campsite when he rode in. He dismounted, and that was when he heard the click of a gun hammer behind him. "Who are you, and what do you want?" asked the man behind Rufus.

"My name is Rufus Sanger, and I'm on my way to Cowtown to send a telegram to my boss. I'd appreciate it if you would lower that gun so we can talk."

"All right, but don't you get any notions about pulling that pistol. I won't think twice about shooting you. If you have a cup, I've got enough coffee for the both of us."

Rufus flipped up the top of his saddlebag to get his cup. When he turned around, he had his gun in his hand with the hammer cocked back. "Well now, friend, the feeling is mutual regarding killing. If you buck me, I won't think twice about putting a couple of slugs in you."

"I see. Then we'll have a cup of coffee and get acquainted. I'm Walter Hicks from down Indian Territory way. You on the run or just passing through?"

"Like I said, I need to send a telegram to my boss, but I might also have someone on my trail. Just not sure, and I really don't care."

"Why would someone be after you?" asked Walter.

"You ask a lot of questions. How about we drink our coffee and talk about the weather or something," said Rufus.

"Yeah, you're right, it's none of my business what you did. But just so you know, two brothers are on my trail for slaughtering their wives and kids."

Rufus took a drink of his coffee and said, "That's

not my problem, and I don't care what you did or who's after you. But if they come here, I'll shoot to kill."

"Maybe we ought to team up together and see how that goes. I had a crew a few weeks ago, but they got slain by those two. When we get to Cowtown, you talk to your boss about hiring me on as your partner," Walter said.

"I'll think about it. My boss is an important, powerful man who's particular about his hired help. We can ride together to Cowtown, and then I'll think about hiring you," said Rufus. He finished his coffee and got up. "I'm going to stake out my horse and get some shuteye."

"You can tether him by my horse if you want." Walter pointed to the east of their campfire. Rufus removed the saddle and his supplies from his horse, then secured the animal for the night. He returned to the fire, rolled out his bed, and climbed in. Not knowing exactly what to think about his new friend, he kept his gun handy as he slept.

Chapter Seventeen

Sawyer was awake at first light and could still hear the Wilks brothers snoring. They had slept under a tree about twenty feet south of the campfire, but even at that distance, he could still hear them where he lay. Although he had gotten used to noisy sleepers while in the army, now it was a nuisance to him since he was used to sleeping in a room by himself. After a few minutes, he picked up a stick and stirred the coals until they glowed, then added more wood to the campfire to start coffee and cook breakfast.

A fresh pot of coffee sat on the hot coals, gently boiling as Sawyer cut slices of bacon and dropped them in his skillet. Ezra got out of his bedroll and headed toward the river. Sawyer could hear water splashing a few minutes later and figured the man was washing his face.

Joe threw back his covers and said, "Good morning, Sheriff! That bacon smells mighty tasty."

"It'll be ready directly after I cook a pan of fry bread to go with it. Ezra is down by the river."

"Yeah, I heard him. That's kind of his ritual—he takes off his shirt and splashes himself with water every morning," said Joe.

Sawyer and the two men finished breakfast and had the last of the coffee from the pot. "I'm heading home when we break camp," said Sawyer. "I hope you fellers find that man you're looking for and get your revenge. This rough, untamed country has little or no law to protect its citizens. Sometimes the only law is what we dish out ourselves."

"Yep, there ain't no lawmen to speak of where we come from, and if there was, they wouldn't track anyone out of Indian Territory. Joe and I will have to have us an eye for an eye when we meet up with Walter again," said Ezra.

Sawyer set down his empty coffee cup. "The killer I'm after wore a black and brown striped shirt, gray britches, and rode a sorrel with two white stockings on its right side. If you come across him on your journey, shoot first and ask questions later. He's a cold-blooded killer who shot the ex-sheriff in the head while he slept. I don't know the man's name, but he works for a high-powered politician in Kansas City."

Joe repositioned himself and lay on the ground with his arm propping up his head. "How far up ahead do you estimate this killer you're after could be?"

Sawyer picked up his skillet and rubbed some sand around inside it to soak up the grease. "At least a day, probably more. I figure he should be in Cowtown by tonight or early tomorrow. After that, it'd be impossible for me to find him, especially if he changed clothes."

Ezra put a good-sized portion of leafy tobacco in his

right cheek. "We'll be on the lookout for him. If he shows up where we are, I'll kill him for you."

"Thanks, I'd appreciate that. I live in Humboldt, Kansas—stop by if you men ever make it east of here." Sawyer got up and started putting the few provisions he had left in his sacks. He saddled his horse and loaded his things, then went to the two Wilks brothers to shake their hands. "I pray you kill Walter for what he did to your families," said Sawyer, and swung up into the saddle.

"You take care, lawman. Maybe we'll see you when this is over," said Ezra.

"I'd like that." Sawyer tipped his hat and rode off.

He wished he had caught up with Sheriff Kiser's killer, but as he'd told Ezra and Joe, once the man made it to Cowtown, the odds of finding him went way down. He could hide out and catch a train and go to Kansas City, and no one would even know that he had left. The best thing for Sawyer to do was to go home and start reviewing documents to put a case together against Senator Bass.

Once he was across the Fall River bottoms, he increased the speed of his horse. A few hours later, he approached an east–west road and took it, hoping it would lead him closer to home.

Around three that afternoon, he stopped beside a creek to rest his horse and let him drink. Sawyer sat with his back to a tree and watched a rider come up to water his horse. The man looked at Sawyer and nodded his head before he dismounted. Sawyer pulled one of his guns and cocked the hammer while the man stood beside his horse and watched it suck up the water.

When the man turned around, he said, "I'm on my

way to Indian Territory. The name's Lester Cobb. I've been on a cattle drive to Cowtown."

"I'm Sheriff Sawyer McCade from Allen County. It's nice to meet you, Lester, but you're a little off track for Indian Territory; it's south of here."

"Yes, sir, but I'm heading to the far northeast side of the Cherokee Nation Cooweescoowee District. I plan to raise cattle there. I'll ride through southeast Kansas and southern Missouri to get there. I have a Cherokee wife waiting for me."

"If you ride about twenty-five miles southeast, you'll find a couple of trading posts if you need any provisions. But after that, I'm unfamiliar with the land you'll be traveling over." Sawyer stood up and put his gun back in its holster. "I best be going. I still have a far piece of riding today. Be careful out here on the trail."

"Thanks, Sheriff. It was nice meeting you."

Chapter Eighteen

Rufus and Walter rode into Cowtown at eight that night to find all eight saloons booming with business. There were no empty places to tie up their horses along the main street.

"Let's ride on through town and see if there's someplace we can sit down and eat supper," said Rufus.

"I thought we might want to go on to one of the saloons and have a few drinks to settle the trail dust," said Walter.

"Listen, if you want to work for my boss and me, then there are a few things you need to know up front. We ain't going to spend time in a saloon and risk getting shot. You'll follow orders, and if I tell you to kill a man, I expect you to do it. Is that understood?" asked Rufus.

"Yeah, I understand. That ain't a problem for me. But I do like to drink and kick up my heels and love on the saloon girls occasionally."

"There's a grub house over there on the right," Rufus said. "We'll get some food, and then I'll find someplace for us to sleep. You can do whatever you want tonight, but come tomorrow, if you're hired on by my boss, you will have to do what I say, or I'll kill you."

He could tell that Walter was not used to anyone talking to him that way, but that was how it would be if he went on Senator Bass's payroll. The senator didn't put up with anyone who didn't pull his weight or who spent all his time drinking and carousing with women.

The two men ate at the café, and when the waitress came to take their plates away, Rufus asked, "Is there a good place where we can rent a couple of rooms for a few days, away from all the noise coming from the saloons down the street?"

"Yep," said the waitress. "There's a hotel on the north edge of town that is kind of out of the way. The cowboys that come in with the herds don't usually stay in that part of town. Dennis and Glenda own the place, and they would be more than glad to have guests." She picked up their plates and hurried back to the kitchen.

When she returned carrying a coffee pot in one hand, Rufus gave her money to pay for the meals. "Could you also tell me where the telegraph office is?"

"Yes, sir, it's on the next street over to the east, by the town center. He's probably still open since two herds came in today. He tries to accommodate the cattle buyers in case they need to send messages."

"Thanks," said Rufus, and stood up. "Come on, Walter, let's go find the telegraph office and see if it's still open before we get rooms."

They rode down the street, and Walter spotted the telegraph office first. When both men were on the ground, Rufus said, "You stay out here and watch our stuff, and I'll be back directly." He didn't give Walter time to reply as he walked up to the porch and went inside.

"Howdy, sir, do you need to send a message?" asked the clerk.

"Yeah, where's something to write it on?" asked Rufus, looking around.

"I'm so sorry, it's usually right here on the counter. I'll get some more."

He returned from a back room with a stack of lined paper, handing a sheet to Rufus, who began to write his message. "I'll be back tomorrow to get my reply," said Rufus, handing the clerk his paper. "You make sure that you keep your mouth shut about what I send and what I receive back."

"Oh yes, sir, confidentiality is a must in this job. I would never say one word about someone's messages."

Rufus went outside and said, "Let's go find that hotel and get a couple of rooms."

"I hope they don't cost much. I'm a little low on money right now," said Walter.

"I'll pay for the rooms, and if you get hired, I'll give you a small advance so you have some carrying-around money," said Rufus.

"That's mighty nice of you," said Walter, tipping his hat to Rufus.

Rufus rented two rooms at the hotel that were situated on the second floor across the hall from each other.

As he paid the entire bill up front, Rufus asked the hotel owner, "Do you have hot baths here in the hotel?"

"Yes, sir, we have two large bathtubs, and I can start heating some water if you require a bath tonight," said the man.

"Yeah, I want a hot bath. Walter, do you want a hot bath also?"

Walter thought for a second and nodded. "I think a hot bath would do me a world of good right now."

"I'll get the water hot. It shouldn't take more than fifteen minutes, if you want to put your things in your rooms. I also have some good cool chalk if you want a jarful while you soak. It's only twenty cents each."

"That would be great. We could use something to drink tonight since we've been on the trail so long," said Rufus.

Both tubs were in the same room, and when they were finished with their beer and baths, Rufus said, "I'm ready to go to bed. What you do tonight is up to you. Tomorrow morning I expect to have a telegram with our instructions. We'll eat breakfast and then do whatever we're told by the boss."

"I'm going to turn in as well. The hot bath and beer have made me ready to get some sleep," said Walter.

Rufus was not one to rise at the break of dawn. He had spent most of his adult life getting up between seven and eight o'clock. The following morning was no exception. The bed was nice and comfortable—something that wasn't a privilege out on the wilderness trail.

When he finally woke up, he started his day by splashing water on his face in the washbasin. A moment of reflection in the mirror, looking at his sandy hair, green eyes, and stubbled gray and brown whiskers gave him an idea. Only a few people had seen him riding through the countryside at Humboldt, looking for the judge and sheriff. This might be the time to grow a beard, so no one would recognize him if he had to return to Humboldt for some reason. He would have to wait on his orders from the senator before he went anywhere or did anything. Who knew, Senator Bass might not be finished with Humboldt and want Rufus to kill the sheriff.

Rufus had been on Senator Bass's payroll for the past ten years. He kept a low profile and stayed out of the limelight so no one would suspect who he was or what he did. Being responsible for eliminating Senator Bass's adversaries in business and politics was reason enough to stay out of the saloons and avoid standing out in a crowd. In contrast, he pretended to be a man who minded his business and didn't cause trouble.

Rufus knocked on Walter's door, but no one answered so he went downstairs to find the hotel owner sweeping the floor. "Have you seen the man who checked in with me last night?"

The hotel clerk stopped working and pointed south. "Yes sir, he said to tell you that he would be at the café having his coffee."

"Thanks. I'll be back later to let you know if we need those rooms another day or so," said Rufus.

"Thank you so much. Do you want your beds made, or should we wait until we hear from you?"

"Just wait. I'll be back later." Rufus walked out onto the boardwalk and stood looking down Main Street for a few minutes before going to the café. Even though the city was small in comparison to Kansas City, he still would take the town over country life.

Chapter Nineteen

After riding hard all day, Sawyer finally came to the Neosho River around six that evening. At least that was what he guessed the time to be. He made a mental note to buy a pocket watch the next time he saw one in Humboldt or Iola.

He wasn't familiar with this particular road that happened to have a bridge that spanned the river. He couldn't remember any wooden bridge before the war. He thought for sure that the road he was on would eventually take him to Iola.

When he tried to ride across the wooden structure, his horse acted up, so he dismounted and led him across the length of the bridge. The horse's chest muscles were twitching once they had made it across, and Sawyer figured that was from the fear of never having walked across a bridge before. He let the scared animal eat grass and settle down for thirty minutes before he mounted up and continued his journey home.

Around seven-thirty that evening, he stopped a man with a wagonload of wheat on the road. "Excuse me, sir,

I'm Sheriff Sawyer McCade from Humboldt, and I'm unfamiliar with where I am. Can you tell me how far it is to Iola?"

The man tied the reins to the wagon's hand brake and stood up. "Hi, Sheriff. I'm Robert Rhea, and I have a farm down the road a piece. I live in Allen County, and me and my boys voted for you. We were delighted that you won!"

"Thanks for voting for me," said Sawyer.

The man pointed down the road. "All you need to do is stay on this road for another three miles, and it will take you to Iola. I reckon you know the way to Humboldt from there, right?"

"Yes, sir, I sure do. Now that you've told me how far it is to town, I can find my way. Be careful out here. If you ever need me, all you have to do is send word."

"I will, Sheriff, thank you."

Sawyer tipped his hat. "Thanks again."

He started around the wagon, but the man stopped him. "Hold on. I was in Iola earlier today, and a Union patrol was in town looking for you. Everyone knows that you fought for the Confederacy, and it got me wondering what they wanted with you."

"I have no idea, but I appreciate you giving me a heads-up about them."

"I'll see you around, Sheriff," said Robert as he picked up the reins and slapped them on the rump of his mules.

What the man had said bothered Sawyer. What did a group of Union soldiers want with him? Maybe they were in town because they were looking for a deserter and wanted his help. But they could have talked to Deputy Craig, who would have helped them. He rubbed his hand over his mouth. He couldn't remember breaking any laws after the war except for robbing the bank, which was no reason for the army to be after him.

Sawyer decided to turn off the road and ride west of Iola, hoping he wouldn't run into any soldiers. He would stay away from Humboldt and proceed directly to his sister's farm south of town. It was possible that they had lookouts watching her house. But why would they do that if he hadn't done anything wrong? This was all getting crazy, and he needed to get to the bottom of it. He would talk to Nancy and see what she knew about the situation.

His plan would be to ride around the farm and approach the back of the barn. Since it would be after dark when he arrived, he could look for campfires in case anyone was camped close to her house. Another option would be to bunk out close to her farm for the night and wait to speak to her first thing in the morning. He thought about it as he left the road and turned west to bypass Iola.

Only a few people would be along the Neosho River's banks this time of night, so he rode along the river until he was a mile from Humboldt. After that, he turned east and continued another mile before riding to the back side of Nancy's farm. It was so dark that he had to guess at where the house and barn were located. He let his horse carry him at a walk while he held one of his pistols in his hand. No campfires were visible in the dark, which was a good sign that, most likely, no soldiers were watching her house.

He tied his horse fifty feet behind the barn and went in on foot. The first stop was the barn, to make sure no one was using it to hide in. It was empty, but he could tell by the way hay was scattered on the floor that someone had been searching the place. He almost tripped on a pitchfork that had been hidden in the hay. They must have used the tool to poke around to ensure someone wasn't hiding in the straw. Were the troops really searching for him, thinking he was a wanted criminal?

With a gun in his hand, he walked to the back of the house and looked in the kitchen window. Everything looked as it should, so he lightly tapped the glass with his forefinger.

He saw movement as he peered through the window, and then Nancy came to the door with a rifle. "Sawyer, is that you?"

Sawyer stood beside the back door. "It's me. Open up."

She pulled the door open, and he swiftly came in and positioned himself so he couldn't be seen by anyone that could be watching the house. "What's wrong, and why is the army looking for me?"

"We need to turn out this light and go in the other room so we can watch the lane just in case they come back tonight." She leaned over the kitchen counter and blew out the kerosene lamp. Sawyer followed her to the dining room, where they sat in chairs positioned toward the window at the front of the house.

"Tell me what's been going on since I've been gone."

"Two days ago, a patrol of twelve soldiers came to town and surrounded the jail, looking to arrest you on treason charges against the US government for not laying down your arms after the war."

"This has got to be a mistake. I didn't lay down my

guns when the war was over. It wasn't mandatory that I give up my guns, I just got on my horse and came home and have done nothing since the war against the government."

"I spoke with Brother Toliver today, and he thinks there is more to this than what they're saying. This morning, he sent a telegram to his friend in Topeka, inquiring about the charges."

"Oh my goodness, I know what it is," said Sawyer, putting his head in his hands.

"Well, spit it out, so we both know," said Nancy.

"I have proof that the big money man behind everything that has been taking place in Humboldt is Senator Bass in Kansas City. I bet he's contacted the army to bring me in on trumped-up charges in order to get back at me for tearing down his little criminal empire here. He's probably paid someone at Fort Riley to come after me," said Sawyer.

"I heard in town that those troops are from Fort Riley, so that very well could be it. I overheard a conversation at the café today between some soldiers. Captain Daniel Whittenhall, the commanding officer at the fort, is in charge of the soldiers," said Nancy.

"That makes sense. It's so close to Kansas City that the senator probably has the captain on his payroll, and there isn't much I can do about it." Sawyer got up, stood beside the window and looked out into the darkness.

"You need to talk to Reverend Toliver tomorrow and see if he can help. You may not know this, but he's acquainted with some important people at the state capital," said Nancy.

"Okay. There's not anything we can do tonight, so I'm going to take care of my horse and get some sleep. I want you to do your usual things in the morning, like I'm not here, and then go to work. I'll leave by the back way and enter town around eleven. If my conversation with the preacher goes well, I might play a little game of cat and mouse with the army boys."

"Oh, Sawyer, don't do something that will get you in more trouble."

"It'll be fine, sis. I'll just play with them a little. Now, you go on to bed and get some sleep."

Chapter Twenty

Rufus walked toward the café and window shopped along the way. He lowered his head and touched the brim of his hat whenever he passed a lady, so they couldn't see his face.

Walter was sitting at a table along the far wall and put his hand up to get Rufus's attention when he came through the door.

"Don't put your hand in the air. It draws attention to us. I don't want anyone to remember us after we're gone."

"You're kind of jumpy this morning. Did you not sleep well in your bed?" asked Walter.

The waitress came over with a cup and coffee pot. She set the cup on the table and used both hands to hold the pot as she poured. "Are you ready to order breakfast now?" she asked, looking at Walter.

Rufus butted in. "Yes, we are ready. Do you have any flapjacks and syrup?"

"No, but we do have bacon, ham, taters, eggs, and

biscuits," said the waitress, moving her hair out of her eyes.

"That would be excellent. Could I get my eggs scrambled?" asked Rufus.

"Yeah, how many do you want?" she asked.

"I'd like six," said Rufus.

"I'll take the same as him," said Walter, pointing to Rufus.

The two men ate their meal, and after Rufus paid the waitress and gave her a tip, they walked outside where he pointed to an alleyway. "We'll cut through here and go to the telegraph office to see what the boss says."

Sure enough, he had three messages when he inquired at the office. He took them outside, sat on a bench and read each one in order of when they were sent. The first message said that Walter would start on the payroll at fifty dollars a month, and if he did what he was told, he would get a raise after two months.

The following message said they should stay put and out of sight but be ready to leave on short notice.

The third message said troops were in Humboldt to arrest the new sheriff. They were to stay close and check for orders often.

Rufus reread each message for clarity while Walter waited on him. Then Rufus shared his news. "You're on the payroll at fifty dollars a month," he said. "And if you do what I tell you, I'll increase your pay. But for now, we're to lay low until further notice. That means you can't be out drinking and messing with women," said Rufus.

"Can I get a little advance on my pay? I'd like to buy new clothes, maybe get a haircut and a shave."

"Sure. I need some new things also, so how about we get haircuts first? I'm going to let my beard grow out. Then, when we finish, we'll buy some new clothes."

"That sounds good to me, boss," said Walter.

An old man and woman were walking by, and Rufus stopped them. "Excuse me, could you direct us to the barber shop?"

The woman spoke up. "Sonny, there's one to the north about a block and three more south of the Lucky Lady Saloon. I would suggest the one to the north. Those others are usually crowded with cowboys coming off the cattle drives."

"Thank you, ma'am," said Rufus, and tipped his hat. He and Walter started walking north and the wind picked up from the south, bringing the smell of cow manure into town.

"I hope the wind changes direction soon. I'm not fond of the smell from those cattle back there," said Walter.

"Yeah, I'm not either. Hopefully we can't smell it inside the barber shop."

The barber kept asking questions and tried to make small talk until Walter finally told him that he wasn't in the mood to talk. When the man started to chat with Rufus, he answered the barber's questions, but the answers were all lies. Rufus liked to mess with people and make them believe the most outlandish stories. He told the barber he was a riverboat gambler and intended to open a gaming hall. It would feature high-stakes poker games, a concert hall with dancing girls, and rooms for the girls to entertain. The barber bought his lie hook, line, and sinker, and Rufus was proud of his skills.

Their next stop was at the mercantile, where they picked out new clothes, and Rufus picked out a new hat to go along with his things. He'd never worn a cowboy hat before, and that would help with his disguise.

Chapter Twenty-One

Sawyer wanted to avoid being seen anywhere near Nancy's place, so he used the barn's back door to mount up his horse, facing the back of the property. He left the farm the same way he came in the night before and traveled the back trails until he got to the road to Humboldt. After leaving the horse in the trees out of sight, he hid along the edge of the road and watched two soldiers on horses positioned beside the road, whose job it was to keep an eye on everyone coming into or going out of Humboldt.

Sawyer returned to his horse, backtracked until he was farther away from the soldiers, and traveled another half of a mile through fields and meadows west toward town. He again rode toward the road and left his horse hidden before walking to the edge of the path and looking in both directions. This section of road seemed safe, so he retrieved his horse and continued traveling toward the river. When he was within eyesight of the roofs of the buildings in town, he veered off toward the river where he could get to the preacher's house.

Sawyer was about a hundred yards away when Reverend Toliver looked up from splitting kindling for the cook stove and spotted him coming. The reverend looked around and then raised his hand for Sawyer to stop. Sawyer halted his horse and watched the preacher go to the back wall of his house and take down a cane pole used for fishing. Sawyer could tell what the man intended, and he waved his hand, turned his horse, and rode back toward the river.

Fifteen minutes later, he heard someone approaching his location through the forest. His fighting instincts kicked in, and he pulled one of his guns, then found a large tree to hide behind. He let the preacher get all the way to the river's edge before he made his position known. "Howdy, Reverend, it's good to see you. I suppose your house is being watched?"

"Hello, Sawyer. I don't know if they're watching mine in particular, but the soldiers are looking for you all over the countryside."

"Yeah, I saw some of them on the road past Nancy's house on my way here. She tells me you might have some valuable information I can use."

"I believe I do. This is a telegram I received this morning." He handed it to Sawyer.

When Sawyer finished reading the message, he returned it to the preacher. "So the judge wants me to come to Topeka by train, and he'll take care of my pardon. Is that the way you read this?" he asked the preacher.

"That's the way I read it. You can ride to Neosho and catch the train there. I'm sure they have soldiers at Iola looking for you, so you may want to bypass it. If you can get on the train tonight, you could be in Topeka the day after tomorrow. Judge Delahay is more than a friend. He's also my kin on my mother's side of the family. You can trust him when he says that Senator James Lane already has a few pardon papers signed by the president in his possession and will give one of them to you. Also, you should take all the evidence you have on Senator Bass with you. Sawyer, I don't know if they will pursue an investigation on the senator or not, but showing them what you have will go far in clearing you of any trumped-up charges."

"I agree. I'll leave out in a few minutes. Where are all the soldiers staying here in town?"

"The captain took over the first cells at the jail, and his men are camped in the open field on the east side of the courthouse. I suspect that the captain is on Senator Bass's payroll, or the senator has put a bounty on your head. Either way, the man is not leaving until he has you in custody or dead."

"You're probably right. If I follow the river or stay close to it, won't that take me to Neosho?" asked Sawyer.

"Yeah, but if I was you, I'd take the main road from Iola to Neosho instead. That way, you'll get there before dark, and you can get on a train today. I'm sure you'll have to change trains at some point down the line, but I don't know where."

"Thanks again for helping me. Could you please let Nancy know what's going on?"

"Sure thing! Now you get going."

Sawyer took off north up the river, and when he crossed over the road, three soldiers came out of the trees with their guns drawn. "You hold it, mister. We have orders to bring you in dead or alive."

Sawyer raised his hands. "I ain't going to try anything. I know you men are just following orders."

"Corporal, go remove his guns and tie his hands together," said one of the soldiers.

They led Sawyer and his horse back into town and as they were in the process of putting him in one of the jail cells, the corporal hit Sawyer in the face and stomach with his fist, all the while laughing and spitting curse words at him about being a rebel soldier. Sawyer tried to protect his face, but it didn't do much good since his hands were tied. Finally, the other two soldiers grabbed hold of his arms, pulled the corporal off him, and put Sawyer in one of his own jail cells. Two soldiers stayed on guard while the third took his horse to the livery.

"You men know that those charges against me are trumped up, and I'm being railroaded over nothing, right?" asked Sawyer.

"You need to shut up. We just follow orders. Captain Whittenhall is in charge. You can plead your case to him when he arrives."

Sawyer sat on the cot with a busted lip and blood seeping from his nose, trying to consider his options. But it wasn't long before gunshots rang out in the street outside the jail. Both soldiers grabbed their rifles and headed out the door to see what was going on. Deputy Craig Martin came in through the back door. "Sheriff, I'm busting you out. Your horse is tied to the hitch rail on the next street behind the jail."

"Thanks, Craig. You probably saved my life." Sawyer gave his deputy a big hug and when he let the man go, he grabbed his guns off the desk and took off out the back door. Deputy Craig followed Sawyer outside.

"Get away as fast as you can. Those soldiers will be coming for you," said the deputy.

"I'm forever beholden to you for taking a chance and breaking me loose," said Sawyer. "You had better get out of here too. I'm sure they'll suspect it was you who freed me."

"Don't worry about me. I have that covered."

Sawyer ran to his horse, mounted up and headed north along the river as fast as his horse could run, and kept at that pace for a fair distance. He wanted to put miles between his position and the soldiers. He stayed in the timber along the edge of the fields until he rode past Iola. After that, he was able to get back on the road and lope his horse the rest of the way to Neosho without encountering any more soldiers.

When he arrived in town, he took his horse to the livery. "I'll be gone for a few days. Could you care for my horse until I get back?"

"I sure can. It'll be two dollars a day for feed and boarding," said the hustler.

Sawyer handed him ten dollars. "Thanks. If I'm gone longer, I'll settle up when I return. If I come back early, you can keep the change."

"Fair enough. I'll take good care of him."

Sawyer walked to the depot ticket counter. "Howdy, I'd like a ticket on the first train to Topeka, Kansas."

"I have a freighter leaving here in one hour if you want that. It has one passenger car," said the ticket agent. "The arrival time in Topeka will be two o'clock tomorrow afternoon. However, this car is not comfortable at all. It has wooden seats and no padding."

"That's fine. Book me a seat."

"Yes, sir, that will be $3.85."

Sawyer paid the ticket agent and took his ticket. "Where is a good place to get something to eat before the train leaves?"

The man pointed across the street. "Go over there and get you something to eat. You should have the waitress pack some sandwiches for the trip since the train has no food service. If you have a canteen, fill it before you go. If you don't have one, they sell jars at the café."

"Much obliged for the information," said Sawyer, and he went across the street.

Chapter Twenty-Two

When Rufus and Walter left the mercantile store, they each had a package in hand. Rufus had on his new hat. It was his first cowboy hat ever, and he already liked it.

As they ambled down the boardwalk to return to the hotel, Walter suddenly dashed into a ladies' dress store. Rufus looked around, bumfuzzled at his partner's odd behavior. He saw two grizzled-looking men riding down the street, but that didn't concern him. He went into the store to see what Walter was doing.

"Have you gone crazy, rushing in here for no reason?" asked Rufus. "I already told you that I don't like to draw attention to myself, and you barging in here has everyone in this store looking at us funny."

Walter stuck his head out the door long enough to look down the street in the direction the two men had gone. "Those fellers that just passed by want to nail my hide to a wall, and they ain't scared to start shooting out in the street."

"It looks like they're gone for now, so let's get out of here before we cause more confusion with these lady folks. You can tell me all about it when we get to our rooms and change into our new duds," said Rufus.

They made quick steps to the hotel to try on their new clothes. Walter came to Rufus's room and knocked on the door.

"Come in and have a seat so you can fill me in on those two men. I need to know if they could hinder our plans."

"Me and a couple other men raped and killed their Indian wives and kids. Those two have hounded me all over the Territory since they found their kin dead. They killed my men at a settlement about thirty miles north of there at a settlement that's south of the Cimarron River, but I had gone home with a soiled dove to have some fun. When I heard what they did to my men, I lit out of there and acted like I went to Coffeyville, Kansas. I guess they figured out I didn't go there, and now they're here to cause me trouble."

"Well, this is an unfortunate situation you've involved me in. Since I like you, I'll let it pass, but those two men must be eliminated. I can't have anyone on our trail or knowing who we work for, so here's what we'll do."

Rufus got up, walked to the window, and gazed down onto the busy street. "You'll stay in your room out of sight from everyone. And I mean everyone, is that clear?"

"Yeah, boss, but what about getting food?"

"Just listen. Until they're dead, I'll bring you food. What are their names?"

"Ezra and Joe Wilks. Ezra is the oldest and largest of the two. Both of them are cold-blooded killers. Joe cut one of my men's throats while he was doing his business on the outhouse hole. He could have waited until he was done and at least had his britches up."

"This is my plan. Joe and Ezra don't know me, so I can follow them to find out where they go and where they stay at night. Then you and I'll sneak up on them and eliminate the threat for good."

"I reckon they'll probably camp out somewhere close to town. I don't figure on them renting a hotel room. They're veteran outdoor frontiersmen and don't depend on anyone helping them," said Walter.

"That's even better for us. We might want to ambush the Wilks brothers while they travel back and forth from their camp."

Walter smiled. "I'm good at ambushing, and I can shoot the eyes off a squirrel at fifty yards with a rifle. We could set up someplace along their trail. You give me two rifles, and I could kill both of them. You could be ready to finish them off if they're only wounded."

"Okay, but let's not get the cart before the horse. First, I'll have to find out where the Wilks stay and watch their daily activities. You stay in your room, and I'll be back later with some food."

Rufus left his room thinking about the chaos that Walter had involved him in. How did he get stuck with these messes? It seemed that he was always the one who had to put an end to bad situations. Maybe he should just turn Walter over to those two men. But then he would have to find another crony to do his dirty work. Walter was more intelligent than his usual help, and he'd come in handy in their fight. Rufus decided to follow his original plan and kill Joe and Ezra Wilks. That way, Walter would be beholden to him forever.

Rufus began his search for the two men, starting at

one of the eight saloons in town. The place was booming with business. Piano music filled the large room with raucous noise, and cowboys danced with the working girls in between tables. Behind the bar was a large mirror with a crack in the top right corner.

Rufus made his way through the bar patrons, careful not to bump into anyone and bring attention to himself. He didn't see the brothers anywhere, so he left and headed to the next drinking hole.

It looked the same as the first one inside, except the bar was on the left wall instead of the right. Again he moseyed through the crowd without seeing the men he was hunting.

By the time he had been through five saloons, he was beginning to rethink his strategy. But then he saw two horses tied to a low limb of an oak tree in a vacant lot next to a wagon yard. Of course, no cowboy straight off a cattle drive would leave his horse like that—a cowboy would leave his mount at the livery or tie it to a hitch post in front of the saloon where he was having a drink.

Rufus strolled down the west side of the street toward the horses, pausing at each storefront to look inside the window for a few seconds. He was almost past a grub hall when he noticed something out of the corner of his eye. He stopped and took a step backward, looking in the window a second time, and sure enough, the two grizzled men were inside shoveling food into their mouths.

Rufus shook his head in disgust. How could anyone have such terrible, unsophisticated manners? Where were those men raised, in a barn?

He crossed the street, found a bench to sit on and

waited for them to come out of the café. Rufus sat with his head slightly down, but his eyes were still focused on the restaurant's door. It took another twenty minutes before the Wilks brothers came out onto the boardwalk, walked to their horses, and mounted up.

Rufus followed on foot when they turned west onto a side street. He took a shortcut between the two buildings and ran down the alley and past two streets until he was ahead of them on the road. Then, out of breath and huffing for air, he hid behind a tree to watch them continue until the street ended, and they rode into the woods.

Rufus headed in the direction they had gone but veered to the north just a tad so they wouldn't think he was following them if they happened to spot him. Walking slow and keeping hidden as much as possible, he spotted their makeshift camp another sixty yards into the timber. They were using two tarpaulins as tents to keep the wind and rain off them. He could hear water running and figured they were camped on the bank of the Arkansas River, which ran through the edge of town.

He kept his distance from their camp but continued to watch them for a while longer. Large trees lined the riverbanks, and after studying the terrain, he knew where he and Walter would kill the two men. It was getting late, and he was tired of walking, so he returned to the hotel after noon time for a nap.

Chapter Twenty-Three

Sawyer stepped onto the waiting train. This wasn't his first train ride—the army had transported him and about three hundred troops from Missouri to Arkansas inside cattle cars about six months after he was trained to be a scout. But this time, his accommodations were much better, even with the hard wooden seats.

The train to Topeka only stopped three times to take on water and coal, and it arrived at its final destination at two in the afternoon, a day after he'd boarded. He disembarked and said to a station hand, "Excuse me, sir, could you direct me to the US Federal Courthouse?"

"Yep. It's about three-quarters of a mile north of here. Unless you like walking, there're buggies for hire out on the street that will carry you there."

"Thanks a lot. That sounds good to me," said Sawyer. He walked out to the front porch that ran the length of the train depot. He was so stiff, and his back was sore from the beating he had taken at the jail. He saw a man standing beside a buggy. "Excuse me, but would you take me to the US Federal Courthouse?"

"That will be four bits unless you want me to wait on you. Then it's a dollar an hour."

Sawyer handed him fifty cents and said, "I have no idea when I'll be leaving, so for now, just get me there."

He was grateful for the ride since he felt like his entire body ached.

He went into the courthouse and saw a large sign on the wall with names and office numbers. Judge Delahay was on the second floor. He found the office with the judge's name on it and after a light tap on the door, he went inside to be met by an armed man sitting in a comfortable-looking chair.

The man stood up and put the short-barrel shotgun in the crook of his arm. "State your name and why you're here."

"I'm Sawyer McCade, and I'm expected."

"Stay put, and I'll announce you."

The man knocked on the private office door and walked inside. He returned in less than a minute. "You can go on in and meet the judge while I get the senator."

"Thanks," said Sawyer, and went inside.

Judge Delahay was a tall, skinny man with gray hair and wire-rim glasses. He stood in front of a large desk and stuck out his hand to Sawyer. "My cousin thinks a great deal about you, young man, and he's informed me of many of the criminal activities in Allen County."

Sawyer shook hands with the man. "Well, to tell the truth, Reverend Toliver is the only man I trust, and I'm blessed to have him as a close friend and confidant. He's helped me through rough times lately and never looked down on me for my actions."

"By the looks on your face, I would have to say that you have had a little trouble lately," said the judge.

"Yes, sir, but it will be fine in a few days."

"My guard Lester has gone to get Senator Lang and US Prosecutor Crozier. We'll take care of this matter of treason as soon as Lang gets here, and after that, you can turn over your evidence and fill us in on what you know. That is, if my cousin told you to bring it like I instructed him to do."

"Thank you, sir. I really appreciate you doing this for me."

There was a knock on the door, and a middle-aged man entered the room. "You must be Sheriff McCade. I'm Senator James H. Lane, and I have papers already filled out for you. All I need is your signature and the judge's signature as the second witness. One document is for the government's records; the others are yours to take home with you."

Sawyer signed his name, and then Judge Delahay signed the papers. Sawyer nodded and shook hands with both men again. "I'm so relieved to get this done," he said. "I was never told that I had to do anything but go home when the war was over."

"There was a communication that went out stating Confederate soldiers could be pardoned if they lay down their arms and took an oath to uphold the laws of the United States," said Senator Lane.

"I'm afraid only a few soldiers did that. Men still need their guns to help feed their families," said Judge Delahay.

Senator Lane put on his hat. "Sawyer, it was nice meeting you. I understand there is still something important you need to discuss with the judge and his prosecutor, so I'll say my goodbye and leave you to it."

"Thanks again, Senator Lane. I'm beholden to you."

"Have a seat while I show the senator out and see if Bobby is here," said the judge.

A man dressed in western clothes and a frock coat entered the room. He went directly to Sawyer, who stood up, and they shook hands. "I'm Bobby Crozier, the federal prosecutor."

"It's nice to meet you, sir."

"Have a seat and tell us everything that has happened in Humboldt since you arrived there after the war," said Bobby.

Sawyer talked with the judge and prosecutor for over an hour, showing them the emails he had and some of his other evidence and telling them the entire story as he knew it. When he finished his comments, the prosecutor said, "We've been investigating Senator Bass and his criminal activities, but this is our first real solid evidence. The man who murdered Judge Elliott and Sheriff Kiser is Rufus Sanger, the senator's number one henchman. He always goes by other names and keeps to himself so no one knows what he looks like. The aliases he likes are Steve Smith and Dan Jones."

"Dan Jones is the name he used at the hotel in Humboldt, and I killed his hired gun. So he is either by himself or has already hired another helper," said Sawyer.

"He always has a hired killer with him to help with the dirty work and who also can take the blame for him if the law gets close. He's not afraid to kill his hired hands or turn them over to the law if it saves his miserable hide," said the judge.

"What do you want me to do about all this?" asked Sawyer.

Bobby stood up and paced in front of the desk while the judge and Sawyer watched him. "Here's what I think. When you return to Humboldt, and Captain Whittenhall sees your papers, he'll make a beeline to the telegraph office to notify his boss. I want you to let him go ahead and send the telegram. You can arrest and lock him up as soon as it's sent. Then send me a telegram telling me he's in custody, and I'll have an army escort come after him."

"What about his men who are also in Humboldt? Won't they try to stand with him?" asked Sawyer.

"Judge Delahay and I will draft you a warrant for his arrest. That way, they have no grounds to do anything but follow orders."

The judge pulled off his glasses and cleaned the lenses. "You'll have to be diligent and watch whoever comes to Humboldt. When Senator Bass gets the telegram from Captain Whittenhall, he'll most likely send Rufus back to kill you and the captain."

"I figured that also," said Sawyer. "I'll tell you straight up that if I see Rufus, I won't go easy on him or the man working for him. They're murderers, and I'll kill them if I get the chance. I wasn't trained to take prisoners."

Judge Delahay cleared his throat. "I'm putting a bounty out on Rufus of two hundred dollars, dead or alive. Now you can do whatever you must, and it's legal."

"Why don't you go get a bite to eat and check on the next train south while we take care of the documents you need to take back with you," said the prosecutor.

"Yes, sir, I can do that. We have a good plan to deal with the murdering horse dung operating in Allen County. I'll be back directly."

Chapter Twenty-Four

Rufus knocked on Walter's door when he returned to the hotel. Walter opened the door with his gun in his hand. "Oh, it's you. I take it you found the brothers in town?"

"I did, and I know where they're staying. They've camped down by the river, and if we sneak down there, we can hide in the timber and kill them both without anyone seeing us."

"Now listen, those two are trail savvy. We'll have to be really careful and not give away our location," Walter said as he sat on the bed and rubbed his face.

"Are you so scared of those men that you don't want to kill them?" asked Rufus, raising his eyebrows.

"No! I ain't scared to kill them one bit. I'm just saying we must be careful and not let them suspect anything."

"Before supper, you and I will walk down toward their camp and find an excellent place to bushwhack those two. You can take one, and I'll take the other. They won't be expecting any trouble today since they just got here. They'll return to town before dark to see if they can find you in one of the saloons."

"If it's all right with you, I'll bring my Sharps and kill one of them with it, then both of us can fill the other one full of lead with our pistols," said Walter. "I'm a dead shot with my rifle."

"I don't care how you do it. You make sure that you hit one of them, so I don't have to worry about killing them both."

"My rifle is with my saddle at the livery stable. We can go there on our way to their camp."

Rufus pulled his pistol from its holster and checked the chamber to ensure it was fully loaded. "Let's go ahead and get your rifle, and then we can hide and wait on those two. They may decide to come back to town earlier than tonight, and I want to be in place if that happens."

"That sounds good to me," said Walter, putting his hat on.

They walked to the livery, and Rufus stayed at the door while Walter went after his rifle. When Walter returned, Rufus raised his hand and said, "Stay where you are. Here they come now."

Rufus moved inside the barn doors and watched the two men. They split up when they got to Main Street, Ezra walking down one side of the street while Joe walked down the other. They were going in and out of the saloons, most likely looking for Walter.

"Come on," said Rufus. "Let's go hide."

The two men hurriedly walked toward the river to get set up for the ambush. "I think we kill them as soon as they walk into the timber," said Rufus. "I'll get behind that big cottonwood tree over there, and you can find a place on the other side of the path, where you have a good line of fire without hitting a tree."

"There's a small clearing between us and their camp. We should shoot them when they're in the opening. That way, nothing can get in the way. You get on one side of the clearing and I'll be on the other, and we'll catch them in a crossfire," said Walter.

"Fine. Let's find a good hiding place, and don't move a muscle when you see them coming back."

Rufus found an old tree that had been blown over some time ago. It was large enough that he could lie on the ground behind it, and no one would see him until it was too late. He figured he would let them pass and shoot them when their backs were to him.

Meanwhile, Walter found three trees that had grown up close together where he could hide. "Hold your position until they get past us," said Rufus. "And then we'll start the party."

Walter nodded. "That works for me. I'll lie down behind these trees and be ready to fire as soon as they pass. However, I do suggest that both of us go ahead and cock the hammers on our guns. They might hear the metal click if we don't do it now," Walter said.

"Okay. I'm going back to my spot and getting ready. I suspect they'll be back to fix supper soon."

Rufus had been in this line of work for years and had developed patience, endurance, and self-discipline. They had been in their locations for about two hours when the sun began to set in the west, and finally he heard voices. With his pistol cocked and ready, the only thing left was to wait behind the tree to let the two men walk by. Walter would also have to be patient. Their plan hinged on them staying diligent until the men had their backs to them.

Rufus held his breath as both men walked past where he lay. They were deep in conversation, and as soon as he had a clear shot, he took careful aim and fired, only to miss the man he'd been aiming for. He fired again, this time hitting Ezra between the shoulders. Rufus kept firing at Ezra until the man was on the ground. He came out from his hiding location to see that Joe was also in the dirt, with blood on the back of his head. Walter ran out with his pistol drawn and went down on one knee to check if the two were dead.

"They're dead. That worked pretty well, didn't it, boss?"

"Come on, let's get out of here in case someone heard the shots and wants to investigate."

"Are we going back to the hotel?" asked Walter.

"I think this calls for a drink at the saloon and then some supper before we turn in for the night," said Rufus. "By the way, you did well."

Chapter Twenty-Five

Sawyer arrived back at the courthouse in Topeka about an hour after he left to get food and a train ticket home. The train would leave at six and it was four now, so he didn't have much time to collect his documents and return to the station. A rented buggy was waiting for him as he finished in the courthouse.

"Judge Delahay, I'm forever obligated to you for helping me out of this jam," said Sawyer. "Bobby, you'll hear from me as soon as I arrest the crooked captain."

"I'll have a detachment ready to come after him. You be very careful and watch your back. I'm almost positive that Rufus will return to Humboldt to finish you off. Senator Bass don't like loose ends—that's how he's survived all these years as a crook," said Judge Delahay.

Sawyer shook hands with both men and left the courthouse. He was glad everything had worked out.

Now all he had to do was enjoy his trip back home, although he wasn't looking forward to the hard seat and rough train ride. On his way back to the depot, he had the buggy driver stop at the café he had eaten at a short time earlier.

"Cowboy, are you ready to pick up your food?" asked the waitress when he entered the restaurant.

"Yes, ma'am, I sure am, and I appreciate you fixing me a sack to take on the train with me. It would be a mighty long ride home without any food," said Sawyer.

The buggy driver dropped him off at the depot and he found an empty seat on the platform where he waited for the train to arrive. It gave him time to reflect on his life and what he wanted his future to look like. He wasn't sure about what the coming days looked like, but he knew he didn't want to be the sheriff for the rest of his life. He'd only run for the job to eliminate the men who had killed his folks, including Judge Elliott and Sheriff Kiser. Everyone was dead who had had a part in the criminal activities except Senator Bass, and it looked like that would be taken care of by the federal authorities.

He was there fifteen minutes when the locomotive rumbled along the tracks, blowing smoke and steam from its stacks.

The conductor came out of the station house and shouted to the guests. "You can board as soon as the train stops. It will only be here long enough to take on water and coal."

Sawyer boarded and got as comfortable as he could on the wooden seats in the single-passenger car. The train left the station and shortly after its departure, a conductor entered the car. "Folks, this train is heading to Kansas City. Once we get there, you'll change to another train that will take you south, and trust me, it will have better accommodations."

The train arrived in Kansas City at ten o'clock in the evening. The station house was huge compared to anything Sawyer had ever seen before. The conductor showed them where to go for the connecting ride to Wichita. The seats in the second train were padded enough that he managed to get comfortable enough to fall asleep.

The following day he got off the train in Neosho and walked to the livery stable to get his horse. He wasn't worried about army troops now, since he had the pardon document in his pocket. The ride to Iola was pleasant, without any sign of soldiers. He continued on, loping his horse to within a mile of Humboldt. That way, his horse would have time to catch its breath in case something went wrong in town and he had to leave in a hurry.

Sawyer sat tall in the saddle as he rode his horse down Main Street in Humboldt. The journey on the train had given him time to plan out what he would do when he arrived. His reason for riding down the middle of the street was to show the town's citizens that he wasn't worried or scared of the troops that had been looking for him. Two army mounts were tied up in front of the sheriff's office. Sawyer wrapped the reins of his horse around a porch post and walked into his office.

Captain Whittenhall was sitting in Sawyer's chair. Another soldier was sitting in one of the other chairs against the wall. Deputy Martin was on a stool close to the potbellied stove, cleaning his gun.

The captain stood up and pulled his Army-issue pistol. "You, sir, are under arrest. Sergeant, remove those guns from his person."

"What charges are you arresting me on?" asked

Sawyer as he stood tall with his official papers in his left hand.

"I'm arresting you for treason on behalf of the US Government for not laying down your arms when the war was over. We ain't putting up with you rebels doing whatever you want," said Captain Whittenhall.

Sawyer handed him the papers. "Before you do something that'll get you killed, I suggest you read these over."

The captain put down his gun and rifled through the documents. "This can't be right. I was told to arrest you. You can't be pardoned. That screws up everything," he said, stomping his foot loudly on the wood plank floor.

Then he turned red and slammed his fist on the desk.

"You should read that last paper very closely. It's a warrant from the US prosecutor placing you under arrest for conspiracy to commit murder." Sawyer pulled both guns. "Deputy Martin, would you be so kind as to open a cell door for the captain?"

Sawyer took the gun from Captain Whittenhall before he took the man by his arm and led him to the open cell.

Sawyer turned his attention to the sergeant, who had stood up during the arrest of his commander. "Sergeant, if you're not mixed up with the captain and Senator Bass, you're free to join your troops and head back to Fort Riley. Another detachment is on its way here to get the captain and place him in the brig for the US federal prosecutor."

The sergeant removed his hat from the hall tree. "I

don't know what he's done or who he's mixed up with. I'm just a soldier that follows orders."

"Then you're free to go," said Sawyer. He looked at Deputy Martin. "I'm going to the telegraph office to inform the US federal prosecutor that the captain is locked up. I'm also sending Senator Bass a telegram in the captain's name, letting him know I've been pardoned."

"Okay. I'm sure after that you'll tell me what all this is about, won't you?" asked the confused deputy.

Before Sawyer could answer, Captain Whittenhall interrupted the conversation. "Don't send a message to the senator. I'll tell you everything if you let me out of here."

"I already know everything. You'll have to talk to the prosecutor if Senator Bass lets you live long enough," said Sawyer.

"I sent him a telegram this morning letting him know I couldn't find you," said the captain.

"Don't worry, I'm going to send him one saying that I'm back in town with a presidential pardon and that you're in jail. I'm sure he'll send his hired guns for us, so I wouldn't get too comfortable in that cell," said Sawyer, smiling.

Captain Whittenhall grabbed the bars with both hands and tried with all his might to make them move. He strained so hard that the blood vessels in his temples became noticeable. "You will sign my death warrant if you send that telegram. The senator will have me killed!"

Sawyer grasped the door handle. "You did this to yourself when you took his money. Now sit tight and think about what you've done."

Deputy Martin followed Sawyer out on the board-walk. "I'll be waiting on you when you get back. Is there anything I need to do while you're gone?"

"No, this won't take long, and then we can talk," said Sawyer.

After Sawyer sent his telegrams, he had Deputy Martin come back outside the sheriff's office, so they could talk in private.

"Senator Bass will likely send his hired killer back to Humboldt to finish off me and the captain. It'll be the same man who was here a few days ago that I went after for robbing the bank and killing Judge Elliott. I'm sure he'll have someone with him since I killed his previous sidekick."

"Do you have a good description of either of them or their horses?" asked Deputy Martin.

"No, but I know the leader's name is Rufus Sanger, and he goes by Steve Smith or Dan Jones. The last I heard, he rides a roan with two white stockings on his right side. I know nothing about the other man that will be with him except he'll be a cold-blooded murderer," said Sawyer.

"When do you think they might get here?" asked the deputy.

"I think tomorrow at the earliest. Here's what I want you to do in the meantime. You go down the east side of the street and tell the cafés, hotels, and saloons to be on the lookout for two strangers. Shouldn't be too hard, since we don't get that many. I'll do the same on this side of the street. If anyone sees them, they need to come find me immediately. We need to have everyone watching for these men."

"Okay. I'll also stop at both livery stables and have

them keep an eye out for the horse with two white stockings," said Deputy Martin.

"One other thing. We ain't taking no prisoners. If you see Rufus or his sidekick, you shoot to kill. Rufus has a two-hundred-dollar bounty on his head, dead or alive," said Sawyer.

"Two hundred dollars is a lot of money these days. I'm sure someone will try to claim it."

Chapter Twenty-Six

Rufus and Walter were on their way to the Wagon Spoke Saloon for a shot of whiskey when Rufus said, "I need to stop by the telegraph office before we have a drink or two."

"While you're doing that, I'll put my rifle back with my things in the livery stable. We can meet at the saloon."

"Okay. Just don't do anything that will draw attention to yourself. I'll be there shortly." Rufus turned north on the street, while Walter kept walking east to the livery stable.

Rufus had yet to decide entirely if he wanted Walter working with him or if he could be trusted. Walter had helped kill the Wilks brothers, but it had been in his best interest to eliminate their threat. So far, he had done all right. The question was, would Walter follow orders when the time came to kill someone who wasn't a threat to him? The one thing he knew about the man was that he was much savvier and wiser than his last partner, Avery. Poor old Avery wasn't intelligent by anyone's standards, but he could be trusted to do his job.

"You have any telegrams for me?" asked Rufus when he walked up to the telegraph counter. He rested his elbows on it and looked down at the seated operator.

"Oh, yes, I do." The operator swiveled his chair to face the desk behind him and picked up a few papers. He pulled out two sheets of paper and handed them to Rufus. "Here's all I have for you right now. That will be two cents for the messages."

Rufus paid the man and read the note that was written on both pieces of paper. When he finished, he went back to the counter. "What time do you close for the night?"

"I close at seven sharp and open at seven sharp in the morning."

Rufus nodded at the man as he looked around the telegraph office and left. He then went around to the back of the telegraph office and checked out the lock on the back door. The office wouldn't be hard to break into so he could use the telegraph key.

Rufus returned to the main road, thinking about his instructions. On the front porch of the leather shop was a bench where he'd seen some elderly men whittling cedar sticks the day before. He pushed some shavings along the ground with his booted foot before sitting down to think about his new orders. The first message had read:

Change of plans, Sheriff gone to Topeka. I fear they will pardon him.

The second message read:

You need to contact me. 9

Rufus knew what the message meant. He would have to break into the telegraph office and send a message to Senator Bass at nine tonight. It also meant that there was a good possibility he and Walter would have to leave soon. It was time for a drink and then supper. He would tell Walter the plan while they ate their evening meal.

Rufus got up and walked down the boardwalk until he came to the Wagon Spoke Saloon. Walter was sitting at a table by himself against the far wall with a whiskey shot in front of him. He waved at Rufus, who shook his head. He'd already told Walter not to do that because he didn't want to draw attention, but maybe the man didn't listen.

A saloon girl came up to their table and smiled.

"My friend needs something to drink," said Walter.

"Honey, what would you like from the bar?" asked the woman. She leaned over in front of Rufus with her hands on the arm of his chair.

"I'll have a whiskey and a beer. Make sure both are in clean glasses. I have a nasty temper if my glasses are dirty," said Rufus, pushing her hand off his chair.

"Yes, sir, coming right up." The woman walked away, swaying her hips for their enjoyment.

"Boss, did you have any messages?"

"Yeah, I'll go over them with you at supper."

The woman came back and placed the two glasses on the table. "That'll be four bits for the drinks." She held out her hand. Rufus gave her the money, picked up the whiskey glass, and drank the shot. He made a face, blew air out of his mouth, and chased the whiskey with a large swallow of the beer.

"Walter, let's drink up and go eat. I have work tonight and must be ready at the designated time."

"What time is that?" asked Walter.

Rufus could tell by the disappointed expression on Walter's face that he wanted to stay and drink. But tonight would be the same as any other night; the big boss wanted something done and they would follow orders and do what they had to, or Rufus would kill Walter. It was simple—Rufus always did what the senator said.

They left the saloon and returned to the hotel before going to the nearest café. The men ate in silence until the server took their plates away. "I have to send my boss a message tonight at nine sharp. We need a crowbar to get into the back door of the telegraph office —you'll need to go buy one. I'm fluent in the telegraph key, so no one will know the conversation between the big boss and me. I feel he'll want us to leave here soon."

"If we have to leave tonight, do you want me to buy some supplies?"

"No, I don't think that will be necessary. After you help me get into the office, go to your room and get packed. I'll meet up with you there."

"Is there anything else I can do?" asked Walter.

"If our orders are what I think, you can go to the livery stable, saddle the horses, and bring them to the hotel. It could take up to an hour before I know what we need to do, so you've got time."

Rufus and Walter sat on a bench outside a women's clothing store, waiting for the telegraph office to close. At seven sharp, the telegraph operator locked the front door of his office and walked away. Rufus and Walter continued to sit where they were until it was dark. Then the two outlaws walked down the alley behind the telegraph office, which was littered with whiskey bottles. A stray dog saw them and ran away.

When they were behind the telegraph office, Walter broke the lock on the back door and left to take care of what Rufus had instructed him to do. Rufus sat down in front of the telegraph key and sent his message at nine o'clock on the nose. He got an immediate reply and wrote it down in the dark. The telegram was long, but he was able to jot down the new instructions. He sent his response and then left the building with a message in his pocket.

Walter was sitting on his bed with his door open when Rufus came up the hotel stairs.

"What are we supposed to do, boss?" asked Walter.

Rufus put his finger to his lips to make Walter be quiet, then motioned for Walter to follow him to his room. The two men went inside, and Rufus laid out the scraps of paper and translated the message.

> *Go to Humboldt and kill Captain Whittenhall.*
> *He failed his assignment and got captured. Then*
> *kill the new sheriff and rob the bank again. You*
> *will be my new man in charge there when every-*
> *thing is done.*

"Who's Captain Whittenhall?" asked Walter.

"He worked for my boss and didn't do his job. From what I get from this, I suspect he's locked up in jail. Let me pack up, and we'll leave tonight," said Rufus.

"My things are on my bed in my bag. I'll go get it and be ready to go," said Walter.

Chapter Twenty-Seven

Once the business owners had been notified about the strangers coming into town, Sawyer walked back toward his office and noticed a nice, shiny black buggy in front of the courthouse. He was almost to his office when he heard his name called out. Sawyer dropped his hand to his gun as he turned to see who it was. A man in a suit with a string tie and cowboy hat walked toward him.

The man stuck out his hand. "I'm John McDonald, the county commissioner here in Allen County."

"Nice to meet you, John," said Sawyer as he shook hands with the man. "What brings you to Humboldt?"

"A few things. First of all, I wanted to meet you and let you know that the new courthouse and jail in Iola are ready for you to move into."

"Oh okay, I was wondering when it would be finished. I heard that a new one was being built before I was elected sheriff," said Sawyer.

"Also, the county has authorized you to hire two additional deputies. Even though we're moving the jail to Iola, we still want to keep a deputy here in Humboldt full-time. So in the future, you'll have a full-time deputy here in Humboldt and two deputies in Iola."

"That's great news, John. Can I start moving prisoners and files to the new jail anytime I want?"

"That's correct."

"Let's talk about these new deputies. Do you have anyone in mind that might want the job?" asked Sawyer.

"I know that Hoss Thomas was a deputy in Wichita before he moved here and started driving a wagon for a freight company. You might want to ask him. He should be at the mule yard in Iola today since the wagons don't run on Wednesdays."

Sawyer stuck his hand back out. "I best go to talk to this Hoss feller today. It's really nice meeting you, John."

Sawyer went to his office to talk to Deputy Martin. "Chris, the new jail is finished in Iola," he said. "The county commissioner just told me we can hire two more deputies. He said a man named Hoss Thomas might be someone I should consider. Do you know him?"

"Yeah, I know who he is. He's a right friendly sort of feller but will fight if someone riles him up."

"You stay here and watch our prisoner. I think I might have a plan for catching Rufus that might work, but first I'll ride to Iola and see if I can hire Hoss as a deputy. Before I leave town, I'll stop by the telegraph office and have the operator send a telegram to the Wichita office and see if it's been broken into. I figure if Rufus broke into the telegraph in Wichita, he most likely has orders to come here and kill Captain Whittenhall. If Hoss hires on, we'll take Captain Whittenhall to the new jail in Iola tonight. We'll then set a trap for Rufus at the jail here, since he won't know that the captain is gone."

"So you're going to set a trap for Rufus," said Craig.

"Yeah, he'll have to break into the jail to kill the captain. We can fix the bed to look like he's asleep. I'll leave the jail and head to the livery stable, but I'll sneak back around and come in through the back door. Then you turn off all the lights and leave through the front door. If Rufus has the jail under surveillance, he'll think that no one is watching Whittenhall and try to kill him. But I'll be waiting on him to make his move."

"That sounds like an excellent plan to me," said Deputy Martin.

"I'll be back as soon as I can," said Sawyer. He headed to the telegraph office and then the livery. When he rode out, his horse was well rested, and it loped almost the entire way to Iola.

Sawyer's first stop was the freight company's mule yard, where a couple of men came out of a small shack to greet him. "Howdy, Sheriff. Can we help you with something?"

"Yes, you can. I'm looking for a man by the name of Hoss." Sawyer knew he was talking to Hoss by the surprised look on the man's face. "It's all good. I wanted to offer you a job."

Hoss removed his hat and wiped his brow with his shirt sleeve, looking relieved. "I thought you were going to arrest me for something."

Sawyer laughed. "Not unless you've done something wrong. I'm Sawyer McCade, and I heard you did some lawman work in Wichita a while back. I need to hire two deputies, and you were recommended to me."

"How much does the job pay?"

"Thirty a month and all the ammo you need."

"That's more than I make here, so I'll take it."

Sawyer shook Hoss's hand to seal the deal.

"When do you want me to start?" asked Hoss.

"I need you to start right now, if that's all right with you?"

"Let me go inside and grab my things. My horse is around the back of the shack."

Hoss rode up and Sawyer said, "Do you know where the new jail is?"

"I sure do, and it's a beauty. Follow me, I'll take you there."

After a short ride, they entered the new jail. It was substantially larger than the one in Humboldt. The office had two desks, six chairs, and a potbellied stove. On the back wall was a heavy wooden door with a square cut out at about eye level, with two iron bars spanning the opening. Sawyer opened the door to find five cells large enough to hold two prisoners in each. At the end of the hall was another wooden door with two locks that could be opened to go outside.

"I told you she was a beauty, Sheriff," said Hoss.

Sawyer went back into the office and removed the badge from his pocket that he'd brought with him from Humboldt. He handed it to Hoss and said, "You go get your gun and wait here until I get back. I'm going to ride back to Humboldt and will bring a prisoner here tonight after dark. I don't want anyone to know he's here or who he is."

Hoss nodded. "I'll keep my mouth shut and bring my double-barrel shotgun back with me, just in case.

Do you want me to set up meals for the guest while you're gone, or do you want to do that tomorrow?"

"Set up anything you think we'll need."

"Okay. I'll unlock the back door for you when you get here."

"Thanks, Hoss. I better be on my way."

Sawyer didn't push his horse on the ride back to the Humboldt telegraph office. He still had plenty of time to change his plan if he needed to. The operator was waiting on him when he stepped inside.

"I have the information you want right here, Sheriff. The telegraph office in Wichita was broken into last night, and they think it happened about nine. Someone walking past on the boardwalk around that time thought they could faintly hear the telegraph key being used. They thought the operator was working late."

Sawyer thanked the operator, rode his horse to the jail, and tied him up by the trough so he could get water. Craig was cleaning his gun when Sawyer came in.

"Did you hire Hoss as a new deputy?" asked Craig.

"Yes, I did, and he's getting everything set up for us. I also learned that the telegraph office was broken into at Wichita last night."

"Do you think he started this way last night?" asked the deputy.

"How far is Wichita from here?"

"It's a good hundred and twenty miles. If they left last night, they would likely get here sometime tomorrow. But of course, that's according to how tired their horses get."

"That's what I'm thinking. We'll take our prisoner to Iola as soon as it's dark and then return here for a good night's sleep. Let's go eat some supper, and then we'll get the horses and head on out."

"What about me? Do I get supper tonight?" asked Captain Whittenhall, holding on to the cell bars with both hands.

"You'll get to eat when we get back from the café." Sawyer moved closer to the cell. "I hope you realize that you're special. I usually don't take prisoners, but being that the US prosecutor wants you and you had nothing to do with killing my folks, I made an exception this one time. If you have thoughts of trying to escape during the trip to Iola, just know I will kill you if you try. Is that clear?" asked Sawyer.

The captain nodded his head. Sawyer and Deputy Martin left to go eat.

Chapter Twenty-Eight

Rufus hated riding a horse, especially in the dark. He was hungry and sleep deprived, and the horse's gait lulled the man to sleep as they trotted along the road. Finally, he gave in to his tired body.

"Find a good place to holed up where we can get some shuteye," he said to Walter. "I can't go much farther."

"Boss, we've only been riding two hours. How about we stop for a break, and you can sleep while I water the horses?"

"Okay, we can do that. I don't know if a short nap will work, but I can at least get some rest."

The road they were on was primarily flat, and when they came to a creek, Rufus's horse followed Walter's down the slope to walk through the water. Unfortunately, Rufus was asleep at the time and fell off his horse, landing at the edge of the creek. Nevertheless, his horse kept walking through the stream and up the other side.

"Hold up," Rufus called out. "I fell off my horse. Bring him back down here to me."

Walter grabbed the horse's reins and led him back to Rufus. "I reckon this is as good a place to stop as any, since you already went to sleep on me," said Walter.

"You watch your tongue. I told you that I was tired. Now look for a place for us to bed down for a couple of hours."

Walter took care of the horses by putting hobbles on their front legs. He then rolled out his bedding and lay down. Unfortunately, Walter was snoring up a storm within minutes of closing his eyes. Rufus couldn't sleep for the noise, so he moved his bed farther away and finally drifted off to sleep.

Rufus was the first one awake the following morning. It was still dark, but the sun would be coming up soon. He got up, rolled up his bedding, and tied it back onto his saddle before waking his partner, who still lay curled up on the ground, snoring.

Rufus put the toe of his boot against Walters's shoulder and woke him up. "You need to get up. It'll be daylight soon, and we need to get going. I want coffee and something to eat at the next place we come to."

Walter lay there for a few seconds rubbing his eyes and face. "Yeah, you're right. We need to head on out." He got up, walked down to the creek, washed his face, and returned.

"Okay, I'm ready to ride," he announced.

With a good night's sleep, the two men were putting distance behind them.

"We've already come a far piece from Cowtown. I figure there should be a trading post or settlement out this way soon," said Walter.

"You'd think so. I sure feel a lot better today after that rest."

"I'm glad you do. The next time we head off somewhere, I'll bring a coffee pot and coffee and some provisions. If we had been able to eat last night, the rest would have been much better," said Walter.

Another mile down the road, they stopped the horses in front of a store. To the store's east were a couple more businesses and maybe twelve houses. Walter took the safety off his gun, and Rufus started to ask why, but instead, he did the same. One couldn't be too careful in a strange place.

When they entered the store, they were met by a jolly woman who smiled and invited them in. "Good morning, gentlemen. Could I entice you with coffee or something to eat before you get your supplies?"

Walter said, "Yes, ma'am, we would love coffee and food."

"Well then, follow me, and I'll fix you right up."

The men finished their food and were on the last of their coffee when Walter asked, "How far is it to the next place that has food?"

"That would be another forty miles," said the woman.

"If you've got some fresh jerky and maybe some more of these biscuits, we'll take that with us to snack on. How much farther is it to Humboldt?"

"That's a full day's ride from here. I suspect you can make it there sometime tonight or early tomorrow morning. After that, it depends on how many stops you make."

Rufus paid for their food, and the two men continued on. When they had ridden another two hours, Walter asked, "Do you want to get there tonight or hole up someplace and get there tomorrow?"

"We still have a lot of miles to travel, so let's keep going and see how we do today. Give me some jerky and biscuits," Rufus said.

It was late afternoon when they stopped at the store the woman had told them about. Their horses were tired, and so were Walter and Rufus.

"Let's water the horses and tie them up by that grass so they can graze a little," said Rufus, pointing to a spot under a large tree. "I'll go in and see if we can get food. A thirty-minute rest will do our horses and us good."

As soon as Rufus stepped into the dimly lit building, he could smell the aroma of food cooking. The man who worked in the place came up to the wooden counter and said, "Evening, stranger. What can I get for you?"

"Is that food I smell for sale?"

"It sure is! Beans and beef with cornbread. I also have chalk to drink if you want to wet your whistle."

"Get two helpings ready. My partner is tying up the horses and will be right in," said Rufus. "How far is it to the next town?"

"The next real town would be Humboldt. It's another three hours from here if you ride hard. I reckon I had better get your food and drink," said the man, and he disappeared into a back room.

After their meal, the two men left the store and got back on the road, walking their horses for another few miles.

"That feller back there said we could be at Humboldt in three hours if we rode hard. We should pick up the pace until our horses need another rest. After that, who knows, they might make it to town," said Rufus.

"Let's not work our mounts too hard. We sure don't want to be on foot," said Walter.

Chapter Twenty-Nine

Sawyer and Deputy Martin delivered Captain Whittenhall to the jail in Iola without one speck of trouble.

Once they got back to Humboldt, Sawyer said, "You go home and get some rest. I'm going to my sister's house and will sleep there tonight. I'll see you in the morning."

"Sure thing, boss."

Sawyer pulled up at Nancy's barn to care for his horse. When he entered the kitchen, his sister was sitting at the table, tapping her index finger on the table-top, waiting for him.

"Brother, sit down and tell me everything that has happened."

Sawyer sat and explained what the preacher had told him and how he'd taken the train to meet with the judge and senator in Topeka. He didn't go into many details, but he did tell her what he suspected would happen next.

"I heard that you got arrested and beaten by those soldiers and then escaped," said Nancy.

"Yeah, but that wasn't nothing. I had help getting away."

"I'm scared for your safety, especially if that horrible man is coming back to town. You better find him soon."

"I want you to take all the money in the bank home with you every night until I find this man. It won't surprise me if he tries to rob the bank again. After tonight, I'll be staying in town until I find him." Sawyer got up and filled a glass with water. "I have something else that I want to talk to you about."

Nancy Lou wrung her hands nervously. "Like what?"

"You know that I backed those men in Texas to gather longhorns. What if I turn our old home place into a cattle-raising operation? I can have the men we hired in Texas drive my cows here, and when Rufus is dead and the authorities have arrested the senator, I can quit the sheriff's job and become a rancher."

She sat looking at him with her mouth open for a few seconds. "Sawyer, you are not a farmer and never will be. But ranching, well, that might be something you'd enjoy. I think that's an excellent idea! You can use this place also because I'm not a farmer either."

"Good. I'll start talking to a few people and see if we can grow grass in the fields instead of crops."

"That's probably a good idea. Otherwise, you'll have to buy a lot of hay to feed them through the winter."

"I'll work on that. There's one other small thing that

I need your opinion on. I met a woman in Clarksville, Texas, that I want to contact and see if she is still interested in getting to know me better. I'd like to invite her to come here if she is. Do you think that's too forward of me?"

"Hmm," said Nancy Lou, giving it some thought. "I don't know. What's her name, and how long have you known her? What makes you think she would still be interested in you after all this time?"

"Her name is Abigail. I did leave quickly, but I asked Kate Jordan to tell her why. I just hope she's not mad at me."

"Why don't you send her a telegram and let her know that you're still alive and thinking about her and then ask if she is still interested in you. Then, if that works out, you can send her a letter telling her how you feel about her."

"Okay, that's what I'll do. Thanks for giving me advice." Sawyer yawned. "We need to get some sleep."

Nancy reached out and grabbed his arm. "Wait. When are you thinking about quitting the sheriff's job?

"Not until the senator is behind bars and Rufus is dead. I promised myself I'd seek revenge on the men who killed our loved ones, and I intend to uphold that commitment. And I promised the good folks of Allen County that as their sheriff, I'd rid our town of corruption. They trust me, and I have to finish this."

"I understand. I want those awful people to pay for what they did too, but I'm also concerned for your safety. I do trust your judgment, however, and I'll stay quiet while you do whatever you need to do. Nothing will stop me from praying for you, so you might as well get used to that, little brother." She got up and hugged Sawyer. "Let's turn in. We both have a busy day tomorrow."

Sawyer left before daylight since he wanted to be in town at first light. He felt in his gut that Rufus would be in Humboldt early. If everything went as planned, Rufus would be dead or in jail by the end of the day.

On his way into town, Sawyer daydreamed about ranching and starting a relationship with Abigail. Hopefully better days were ahead. Today would be the start of a new chapter in his life. He'd send her a telegram and one to Abe Jordan, too, about the cows.

Smoke was pouring from the jail stove pipe when he tied up his horse out front. He entered the building to find Deputy Martin in the first cell, preparing it to look like someone was asleep on the cot.

"That looks mighty convincing."

"Thanks, Sheriff. There's fresh coffee on the stove."

"I've been thinking about Rufus. We should keep watch on the road coming in from the west in case he comes in that way. We might be able to stop him before he arrives in town."

Deputy Martin thought for a moment before he spoke. "The best place to stop him coming in from the west is at the river crossing. He'll most likely use it to get into town. I can hide out there and watch for him if you want me to."

"Yeah, do that, and I'll stay here in town just in case he rides in from another direction."

Deputy Martin grabbed a rifle from the gun rack and left the office. Sawyer sat down and drank his coffee, deep in thought. What would he do if he were coming into town to kill someone? He would approach in a way that no one would suspect. Rufus might take a detour and come in from the north or the south. The north would be the most unlikely direction, so that was where Sawyer decided to take up a position on the edge of town and wait.

Chapter Thirty

Darkness overtook Rufus and Walter with miles yet to travel. They were both tired, and the horses could hardly keep going.

"Rufus, we need to find someplace to stop for the night. Let's look for a light and see if we can spend the night somewhere with soft beds and some food."

"You're right. One more day won't kill us," said Rufus, laughing.

"Yeah, well, sorry that I'm too tired to laugh. Look over there. I thought I saw a light through these trees." Walter pointed west. "There it is again. There's a house back in that grove of oaks. I say we go in, kill whoever lives there, and take over their house for the night."

"I see it now. I'm okay with that if you want to do it."

"If there's a woman there, she's mine for a little fun," said Walter.

"You can do whatever you want. How about I come in from the north, and you come in from the east?" said Rufus.

"I say we ride on in and see what happens. I'm ready for some food and a good night's sleep."

"Fine by me, but have your gun handy in case they come out shooting."

The two outlaws rode within a hundred yards of the house and dismounted to continue on foot. Rufus lagged behind Walter since he was more careful than his partner, who walked right up to the front door and knocked three times with his gun butt. Rufus would hurry closer when the door opened.

Walter knocked on the door again, turned to Rufus, and motioned for him to go to the back of the house. Rufus eased down the west side of the structure and heard voices as he approached the back of the building. He backtracked to the front of the house and made a slight whistle to get Walter's attention. Walter came over to him. "I can hear voices in the backyard. You go around on the east side, and I'll take this side."

Walter nodded and started to the other side of the house. Rufus waited until the other man had turned the corner before going toward his earlier position toward the back of the house. He cocked the hammer on his pistol, then came around the back corner of the house and into the backyard. He took the man and woman by surprise and commenced firing. Walter also fired his gun at the couple.

When the hammer of his weapon landed on a spent cylinder, Rufus said, "Hold up. They have to be full of holes by now."

He went to the man and woman to ensure they were dead. Walter was reloading his pistol and didn't pay attention to the corpses. "What do you reckon we should do with them?" asked Rufus.

"Don't matter to me, since we killed the woman. But I ain't digging no hole in the ground. I'll go get the horses while you ponder what to do." Walter walked off.

Rufus hated to leave the bodies out in the open like they were. He had a thing about wild animals eating people. It gave him the creeps just thinking about it. He looked around the backyard. There was an outhouse, a chicken coop, and a barn. He walked to the barn to find it empty. A few feet behind the barn stood a corral with two horses. He heard Walter approaching with their horses and went to meet him.

"We can use the horses to drag the corpses into the barn and out of sight. That way, no one will find them for a while," said Rufus.

"I don't have a rope. Do you?"

"There're ropes in the barn. I'll go get one," said Rufus.

They left the corpses in the barn and their tired horses in the lot, fed and watered. Then the men went to the house and inspected their new accommodations for the night. They found two beds and plenty of food to cook, and had themselves a proper supper.

Rufus lay in his bed, all comfortable, thinking about how he wanted to proceed with his assignment the following day. He was a careful man, so they would ride west and ford the river west of Humboldt. Then when they were close to town, he would see if Walter would really be his permanent criminal partner.

The two men slept in the next morning, and the sun was already high in the sky when Rufus heard Walter throwing wood in the kitchen stove. He got up, went outside, and looked around the place to ensure no other houses were in sight.

"What have you found for breakfast?" he asked when he entered the kitchen.

"There's bacon and potatoes. Take a pan and see if there are any eggs in the henhouse. If there is, we can feast before we wreak havoc on Humboldt."

Rufus grabbed a mixing bowl off a shelf, walked out to the chicken pen, and opened the gate. He was met by a rooster with outstretched wings, prancing around ready for a fight. Rufus kicked at the bird, but it jumped up and spurred his leg. Rufus lost his balance and fell backward onto the ground, cursing and grabbing for the chicken as it advanced to fight. The bird kept coming at him as he scrambled to his feet and ran out the chicken pen gate, angry that a stupid rooster had caused him to fall.

He stood, collecting himself while he dusted the dirt and chicken manure off his clothes. Then he saw a shovel leaning against a nearby tree. He would see how much that stupid bird really wanted to fight! He grabbed the shovel and went back into the pen, again being met by the charging rooster. After a couple of hits to its head, the rooster scurried off.

Rufus brought in a pan of eggs and set it on the table. He said nothing about the rooster attacking him, but Walter turned around and said, "What're you doing with chicken crap all over your shirt and pants? Did you fall down in the pen? You stink to high heaven. I think you need to wash those clothes."

"Yeah, I tripped and fell. I'll see if that man we killed has something I can put on for a little while." He

found a pair of bib overalls and wore them while his
shirt and pants dried outside on the clothesline.

They stayed at the house long enough to have their
noon meal. After they'd eaten, Rufus told Walter, "Go
get the horses. I'm putting my clothes on, and we'll
leave."

Chapter Thirty-One

Sawyer rode his horse to the north end of town and tied him to the hitching post in front of Miller's Wagon Repair. He walked across the street and sat on a rickety chair in front of a vacant building. It might be a long wait, so he got as comfortable as he could, even though it was hot and humid in August.

He had time to think about how this had started and what made him become sheriff. He had returned from Texas to get revenge on the men who'd killed his parents and his brother-in-law. He ran for sheriff so he could legally go after the crooked judge and sheriff. Now that they were both dead, he didn't want to continue as a lawman. The jail and courthouse were being moved to Iola, and he definitely wasn't moving there. Instead, he wanted to stay close to his sister and pursue ranching. He needed to contact Abe Jordan to see if he had any cattle and if so, if they could be brought to his family's land. He would also have to find someone to plant grass in the fields and hire carpenters to build a new house and barn since the old ones had been burned.

His mind wandered to the pretty waitress who had touched his heart with her beauty and playfulness. What would he say in the telegram to Abigail in Clarksville? Would she even reply? The only way to know was to reach out and see what she did.

By noon, Sawyer had grown tired of sitting in the heat waiting on Rufus to come into town, so he got on his horse and rode to the river crossing where Deputy Martin was staked out. "Deputy, I'm ready to call this quits and wait until tonight to see if anything happens at the jail."

"I'm with you on that. This sitting goes a long way in making my day. I'd just as soon take a beating than stay out in the heat doing nothing but waiting."

"Mount up, and let's get something to eat. Then we'll reevaluate our plan."

"That sounds good to me. I'm getting mighty hungry," said Deputy Martin.

While the lawmen rode into town, Sawyer asked, "Do you know any farmers I can hire to plant grass on my homeplace and my sister's farm?"

"No, not right now, but I can ask around. Are you thinking about raising cattle?"

"Yes, I am. I also need a carpenter to build me a new house and barn."

"That I can help you with. Benny Sage is a local carpenter you can hire to build whatever you want. If I see him in the next few days, I'll send him to talk to you," said Deputy Martin.

"Great," said Sawyer. "Oh, one more thing. When

this is over with Rufus, I'm going to resign as sheriff, and I recommend that you take over."

"I sure didn't see that coming! I figured on you to be sheriff a long time."

"No, I only ran for the job to get Kiser out of office so I could legally arrest him and Judge Elliott. I came back to get revenge. Rufus is the last one on my list besides Senator Bass, and the government will take care of him. After Rufus is dead, I'm resigning."

"You don't intend to arrest Rufus if you get the chance?" asked the deputy.

"No, he's a murderer. You should know by now that I take no prisoners."

"Yep, I know that. I'll give the sheriff job some thought, but right now I'm hungry, so let's go eat."

Chapter Thirty-Two

The two outlaws had been back on the road for an hour after leaving the house where they had spent the night. Rufus motioned to his right. "Come on. We'll ride west of Humboldt before we cross the river," he told his partner.

They had ridden close to two more miles when Walter's horse stumbled and descended onto its knees, making its rider tumble headfirst to the ground.

Rufus halted. "What in the world is going on with your horse?"

Walter got up. "Thanks for asking if I'm hurt." He walked to his horse, which stood on three legs. Its right front leg was slightly cocked, as if it was injured. Walter took hold of the reins and led him forward a few steps, and then he bent down and felt along the horse's right leg. "He stepped in a hole and probably pulled a ligament or something. I'll try to ride him, but I need another horse soon. He can't go much farther on a bad leg."

"I know where there's a trading post west of us that

has horses for sale. You can ride double with me until we get there. I'm sure you can strike up a deal to trade your pony for a sound one."

"Okay. Let me hand you the reins to my horse until I get on behind you. Then I can lead him."

They started out and had to walk Rufus's horse so the hurt one could keep up with them. It was difficult getting across the river with the two men riding double, and when they were about halfway across, Walter had to drop the reins of his horse so it could cross by itself.

When they were finally safe on the far bank, Rufus stopped his horse while Walter got down and retrieved his mount. Then they took off again and finally reached the trading post on the river by late afternoon. They went inside while their horses rested and got something to eat before they started dickering over another horse.

Rufus could tell that the trading post owner remembered him. The man seemed scared and fidgety. He probably remembered the gun that Rufus had aimed at his face a few days earlier.

"Afternoon, strangers. What can I get for you?" said the man with a tremor in his voice.

"We'd like something to eat and some cool chalk to drink, iffin you have some."

"Yes, sir. I'll get you that chalk while I get the missus to spoon you up some venison stew. I'll be right back if you want to sit at the table over there." He pointed to his right.

When the two men were finished eating, Walter said, "My horse stepped in a hole a little ways back and pulled a ligament in his front right leg. I'd like to trade him for a good mount, and I would be willing to pay some boot since he's hobbling."

"I'll look at him, and then we can talk about trading," said the store owner.

All three men went outside, and the trading post clerk led the horse around, felt his leg, and then said, "He stretched out the ligament all right. He won't be of much use for a month or so. But I'll consider trading for him if we can work a deal. Come on out back and look over what I have."

Walter picked out a black horse that looked to be in good shape. He asked, "How much boot do you want if I take this one?"

The man rubbed his chin as he thought about what to say. "I'll take sixty dollars and your horse."

Walter stood looking at the horse for a few seconds. "I was figuring on fifty dollars and my horse. Mine will be worth a hundred when he's well."

"Yep, and mine's worth a hundred now."

Rufus reached into his pocket and pulled out his money. He handed the man sixty dollars and said to Walter, "Put your saddle on the horse, and let's get on the road. It's getting late."

Walter swapped his saddle over to the new horse. They headed out to the south until they were out of sight and then turned east toward Humboldt.

Chapter Thirty-Three

Sawyer returned to the sheriff's office after he and Deputy Martin finished eating at the café. He had been gathering his thoughts and decided to sit down and write his two telegrams. The first would be to Abe Jordan about the cows, and the other to the sweet woman he was still in awe of down in Clarksville, Texas.

> *I hope this finds you back home. I'm fine and have almost finished that thing I came home for. I want to take up ranching. Was the cattle drive success-ful? If so, how many cows are mine? Would it be possible to buy more cattle from the others? Can the men drive them to Wichita, Kansas?*
>
> *Sawyer McCade.*

He read over the message and, once he was satisfied with it, turned his attention to what he would say to Abigail. He smiled as he thought about her kissing him and ran his tongue across his lips, trying to remember what that last kiss tasted like. If he never saw her again, at least he'd always cherish their short time together.

He began to write, but after a couple of sentences, he wadded up the paper and threw it in the trash. What had him so worried about what to say? He knew she liked him, so he decided to just get right to the point.

I'm in Kansas and missing you. I hope you miss me. Are you still interested in building a relationship together? I sure hope so!

Sawyer

He read the message aloud and realized it didn't sound very romantic. He thought about rewriting it but didn't know what else to say. It would have to do for now. He got up and put the messages in his pocket.

The walk to the telegraph office was quite productive. A man in work clothes and a straw hat came across the street and called out to him.

"Sheriff, do you have a few minutes?

"Sure. Who might you be?"

"I'm Jim McLaughlin, and I do custom farming. Craig said you might be in the market for my services."

"I might be. I want to turn my family farm into a ranch and need meadows for the cows."

"I'll be honest with you, this is not the time of year to start planting grass. How many acres do you intend to graze?"

"The farm is 640 acres, but we only farmed about 390 acres. The rest is timber along the river with some open meadows. I also want to plant grass on my sister's land, but I don't know how many acres it is or how much of it is farmland."

"Since it's late summer, I suggest you plant wheat and let your cows graze it as a supplement. That, along with the grass you have in your meadows, should be sufficient to get a small herd through the winter, especially if you can feed them hay. Then in early spring, when the weather starts getting warm, we can start turning your cultivated land into pastures."

"I tell you what I'd like for you to do," Sawyer said. "Do you know where my folk's place is south of town?"

"I do, and I'm quite familiar with Nancy Lou's place also. I've planted on that ground before when the previous owner lived there."

"If you don't mind, would you ride out to both places, look over the planted crops, and then tell me what you think we should do in case I get cattle and have to feed them through the winter?"

"I can certainly do that. I'll be right over there first thing in the morning."

"Good. Thanks for helping me out, and it's nice meeting you," said Sawyer, holding out his hand to shake.

"It's nice making your acquaintance too, Sheriff."

Sawyer watched the man turn and walk back across the street. Then he continued to the telegraph office. Mr. Hoffman looked up from reading the newspaper, folded it, and laid it on his desk.

"Come on in, Sheriff. What can I do for you?"

"Hello, Mr. Hoffman. I'd like to send a couple of telegrams."

"Sure thing. Give the messages to me." He started to lightly tap his middle finger on the telegraph key.

Sawyer watched, astonished that he could tap a small device right in front of him, and someone hundreds of miles away could understand what it meant.

When Mr. Hoffman was finished, he said, "Sheriff, that will be four bits. When the replies return, I'll bring them to your office."

"Thanks, I really appreciate that. Say, do you know of a good carpenter in town who can build a house?" asked Sawyer.

"Yep, my wife's brother is a top-notch carpenter, and he's not real busy right now if you need some work done. I saw him a little while ago. He was going to the hardware store. You might catch him there. His name is Owen Potter."

"Thanks, I'll go see if he's still there. Much obliged."

Sawyer watched along the street for a horse with two white stockings as he walked along the boardwalk. The door was open at the hardware store, and he could see four men conversing by the counter. One of them must have said something funny because they all laughed.

Sawyer went up to the group of men. "Excuse me, is one of you Owen?"

"I'm Owen," said a short man with a beard wearing bib overalls.

"I need to hire a carpenter to build me a house and barn. Is that something you'd be interested in doing?"

"Yes, sir, I sure would! Let's go outside where these busybodies can't hear our conversation."

"I want a new house and barn built on my folk's property south of town," said Sawyer once they were outside. "If you would like, you can ride out there and look it over, and then we can discuss what you can do for me."

"I think that's a good idea. But if I remember correctly, the place is still a mess from the fire out there. That'll have to be cleaned up before we do anything," said Owen.

"Yep, I'd like you to include that in your estimate."

Owen stuck out his hand. "I'll go on out there and then start on a figure. How many bedrooms are you wanting?"

"Three will be enough for now. As for the barn, it will be used for a cattle operation, so I won't need to store farm equipment. Instead, I'll most likely store hay and grain in there."

"Okay, I'll get back to you in a few days."

"Thanks," said Sawyer, and returned to his office.

Chapter Thirty-Four

Rufus was reminiscing about the last time he was in Humboldt. The new sheriff had entered the saloon and killed his associates and their hired gun hands. The man's name was McCade. Rufus reflected back on all the men he had encountered in his lifetime, and this McCade fellow frightened him the most out of all of them. The sheriff was either extremely brave or stupid. Most likely brave.

Rufus needed a plan to protect himself if things didn't go as planned. "Say, Walter, how do you like your horse?"

"He's all right, I guess. It beats walking in this heat."

"Let's trade horses. I kind of like the looks of your mount," said Rufus as he pulled back on the reins to stop his horse.

"Fine by me, you paid for him, and I've always liked your sorrel."

"Okay then. We'll switch saddles too."

Once their gear was swapped, they were back on the road that led into Humboldt from the west.

"I have a plan when we get to town," said Rufus. "I'm going to hole up out back of the Ellison Hotel while you ride in and get us rooms. I've been there before and someone could recognize me, so you go in and take care of it. Make sure to get us accommodations that allow us to watch the sheriff's office."

"Do you only want to stay there for one night or what?" asked Walter.

"Yeah, one night should be fine. After you pay for the rooms, go to the back door and open it for me. We'll hide upstairs in our rooms and watch out our windows for when the sheriff and deputy leave the jail for the night. Then we'll sneak into the jail and kill Captain Whittenhall in his cell."

"Sounds like a good plan. Do I take the horses to the livery, or is there a pen behind the hotel?" asked Walter.

"Use the hotel's pen. We want our mounts close by in case we need to skedaddle out of here in a hurry. Be sure to let me in the back door. I don't want to be out in the alley too long."

"Okay, I'll let you in and then care for our horses."

"Say, once that's done, go to the café and get us a couple of sandwiches or something to eat. Here's money to pay for the hotel and food. Don't do anything to draw attention to yourself. I want this to go without a hitch."

"You can count on me, boss."

"Good. Let's ride."

Two miles out from Humboldt, Rufus said, "I'm going to veer off the road and come in from the southwest. You go ahead and ride on in, and I'll see you at the hotel's back door."

"Okay, I'll see you in a bit."

Rufus urged his horse to go faster as he left the road and rode through timber and meadows. He had farther to go than Walter, so he kept a fast pace until he could see the buildings in town. He lowered his hat to shield his face from anyone he passed as he rode into town.

The pen behind the hotel was empty when he rode into it. He loosened the saddle's girth strap, removed the bit from his horse's mouth, and left the bridle nearby so he could quickly get his horse ready to go if need be.

He leaned against the hotel wall beside the back door and waited for Walter. He wasn't there for a minute before he heard the lock disengage, and the door opened.

"Come on in. It's clear, and the stairs are right over here."

The two men climbed the stairway to the second floor and went to room number six, which was going to be Rufus's room.

"What number are you in?" asked Rufus.

"I'm next door in number eight."

"Good, now go ahead and put your horse with mine and get us some food. While you're at the café, see if you can find out where the sheriff lives. That might be important to our plan. While you're gone, I'll move that chair by the window and watch the sheriff's office. Tap the door twice and then twice again when you get back, so I know it's you."

"Okay, I'll be back later," Walter said. He went to the door, opened it, looked both ways, and left.

Rufus positioned a chair near the window and looked out onto the street below.

Chapter Thirty-Five

Sawyer had almost returned to his office when he heard his name called out yet again. He turned to see Mr. Hoffman following him, waving a piece of paper. Sawyer retraced his steps.

"Did I get a reply to one of my messages already?" he asked.

"Oh, yes, you did, and it's a doozy."

Sawyer opened the folded piece of paper.

I miss you as well. Yes, I'm very interested.

Abigail

Sawyer folded it up and put it in his pocket. He had a smile on his face that reached from ear to ear.

"Well, it looks like you have a girlfriend," said Mr. Hoffman as he turned and started back to his office.

Sawyer called out, "I sure do, and she's a looker! Thanks for bringing this to me."

He was so tickled that she was still interested in

him that he decided to walk to the bank and share his good news with his sister.

Nancy Lou was in her office when he entered the building whistling a tune. She motioned for him to come in. "What brings you to see me in such a chipper mood?"

"It shows that much?" he asked as he moved a chair closer to the desk and sat down. "I sent Abigail a telegram a couple of hours ago, and she sent one back."

"What did she say?"

"She said that she misses me and is very interested in me."

"Well, now, my baby brother has a lady friend. Congratulations."

"I'm going to wait until I hear from Abe Jordan about the cows before I send her a letter. I asked him if he had any cattle for me and if it would be possible for me to buy additional cows from the other men. Also, I'm hoping they can drive the cattle here. If all that pans out, I'll write her and see if she will move up here."

"Sawyer, I've been doing a lot of soul searching and have decided to sell the bank so I can take care of my baby when it's born. The doctor says that I'm fine and everything is going well, but I don't want the stress of managing people's money to interfere with me and my baby. I want to stay home and raise my child and be your partner in the ranching operation. I get offers every few days from people wanting to buy me out. You turned the bank over to me after you killed Hopson, so I want your opinion on what I should do."

"Sis, I'm totally fine with you selling the bank. I think you can make a good profit off it, and when we get in the cattle business, we'll do fine."

"After those two men robbed the bank a few weeks back, I brought in all the money you had hidden in my barn. Did you realize that you have over thirty-three thousand dollars, and that you are quite well off for a simple soldier who just came back from the war?" She smiled and shook her finger at him.

He knew she suspected where the money came from, but he didn't confirm her suspicions. "The Army paid well, is all I can say," said Sawyer, leaning back and crossing his arms.

"One more thing," said Nancy. "How about you ask Abigail to come on up, and she can live with me. That way, I'll have someone to help me with the baby until you build a house on our land."

Sawyer smiled at her. "I think that's a wonderful idea. I've already talked to a carpenter about building a house and barn on our folks' place. I also talked to Jim McLaughlin, a custom farmer. He'll look at our two places and get back to me on what he thinks we'll need to do to feed the cattle through the winter."

"Who's the carpenter that you talked to?"

"A man by the name of Owen Potter. He's going out to the property to see what it'll cost to clean up the burned debris and build new structures."

"Owen does business with the bank, and he has a good reputation of being a good carpenter from what I hear."

"Mr. Hoffman recommended him to me. Craig recommended another carpenter, but I haven't talked to him."

"There are two sections of land between my farm and our old home place. What are your thoughts about buying them if we can?"

Sawyer leaned back in his chair, removed his hat, and ran his fingers through his hair. "Sis, that's most likely going to cost over twenty thousand dollars. That could put a strain on my bank account with me buying extra cows and having a house and barn built."

"I still think it's very doable. Besides, you could always rob a bank if you need to." She started laughing, and Sawyer just had to take that one on the chin and grin.

Nancy laughed so hard at her own remark that she had to compose herself before continuing. "Seriously, we could go in on them and buy both sections together. That way, you'd have more money to buy even more cattle. I checked, and a person can buy longhorns in Texas for four dollars a head. Once you get them here and fattened up, they'll bring forty dollars at the eastern markets."

"I tell you what. Let's see what Abe has to say, and then we can decide if we want to buy more land and cattle," said Sawyer. He got up. "I best be getting back to the office. I'll let you know when I hear from Abe."

"Okay. You be careful out there. I love you, Sawyer."

"I love you too. I'll see you later."

Sawyer crossed the street when he left the bank and walked along the boardwalk to check the horses tied along the street.

Chapter Thirty-Six

Rufus watched Sawyer walk down the boardwalk, inspecting the horses tied to the hitch rails along the street. Rufus remembered how Sawyer had wiped out an entire gang in the saloon a few weeks earlier. This was a tough man, and he and Walter would have to be careful and either take him by surprise or shoot him in the back. There was no way Rufus wanted to kill him face-to-face.

Then Rufus realized what Sawyer was up to. Sawyer was looking at the horses because the sheriff probably knew his steed's stocking markings. It seemed that Sawyer had been warned that Rufus was returning to town, and the sheriff was watching for him. Rufus laughed. That sheriff would never see him coming. Walter would take the fall if everything worked out right, and Rufus would be long gone since the law would think Walter was him.

There came two taps on the door and then another couple. Rufus had his gun in his hand but remembered what he had told Walter about knocking. He opened the door with his gun cocked in his hand, and Walter came in with a food sack. Rufus returned to sit at the window and ate his fried chicken and biscuits while watching the street.

When finished, he got up, poured water from a pitcher into a bowl, and washed his hands. "Did you find out where the sheriff lives?" asked Rufus.

"Yep, a man that was eating at a table by himself said that he thinks he stays with his sister about two miles southeast of town," said Walter as he started on another chicken leg.

"That will work out just right. I've been thinking about what we're going to do. We don't want to stay in town longer than we have to, so when the sheriff and deputy leave the jail tonight, I want you to get your horse and ride to the jail. First, go inside and fill Captain Whittenhall full of holes. Then, come back outside, mount up, and ride south. I'll be south of Humboldt waiting for the sheriff to come back to town and I'll kill him on the trail."

"You said my horse. Which one is my horse?"

"We traded horses today, so you own my old horse, and that's the one you ride."

"Okay. Where do you plan to bushwhack the sheriff at? I'd like to know so I won't ride past you and meet up with him."

"I'm not sure. I'll be close enough to the road to stop you."

"When do you want me to saddle up?" asked Walter.

"Let's give it another thirty minutes. The sun is setting, so it'll be dark soon."

"In that case, I'm going to the outhouse, then I'll saddle up before I return here."

"Fine, I'll keep watch until you get back."

About thirty minutes later, Walter came back into the room. "Has anything happened yet?"

"No. From what I can tell, they're both still inside the sheriff's office."

Walter sat on the bed, pulled his gun from the holster, and checked the chambers.

"The jail door just opened. Here comes the sheriff walking down the boardwalk to the south."

Walter got up and stood so he could also watch. "I bet he's going after his horse from the livery stable."

They watched Sawyer ride away from the livery a few minutes later and head south.

"There he goes, just like we thought he would. Now we wait on the deputy to leave so I can plug the captain," said Walter.

Rufus sat still and didn't reply to Walter. Twenty minutes later, the kerosene lamps in the sheriff's office went out. Deputy Martin came out the door and walked north.

"Are you ready for me to head out?" asked Walter.

"No, let's give it a few more minutes. While we're waiting, you go down and get my horse ready to travel, and I'll keep watch to make sure one of them don't come back. Then, if you don't hear from me by the time you're done, you go on with our plan."

"Okay, I can do that," said Walter, leaving the room.

Chapter Thirty-Seven

Sawyer rode south from the livery stable until he knew he couldn't see any of the houses or businesses in Humboldt. Then he turned to the west and rode wide around town until he could get close to the backside of the jail—but not too close. He dismounted, left his horse tied in some trees, and stayed in the shadows as he made his way toward the back door of the jail.

Deputy Martin unlocked the back door from the inside when he heard a knock and let Sawyer inside. Sawyer had already placed a chair in the front left-hand corner of the room behind a coat rack opposite the cells so the killer wouldn't be able to see him when he came through the front door.

"I'm going to stand by the door until you turn off the light in case they can see in the window," whispered Sawyer. "There should be enough natural light through the windows for the killer to see the dummy in the cell."

"I'll blow out the lantern, walk north, and turn east on Hope Street. That's where I'll hold up and see what happens." Deputy Martin blew out the lantern and exited the door while Sawyer went to his chair.

Sawyer figured Rufus would give the deputy time to get home before he tried anything. That would give him more time to kill the captain and leave before the deputy could return. Sawyer had at least ten minutes to wait, he figured.

After thirty minutes, Sawyer thought about needing a pocket watch again. But then he heard the creak of saddle leather right out front of the office, like someone was getting off a horse. He pulled his gun and sat still, anticipating Rufus entering through the front door. Sure enough, the door swung open, and a man ran to the first cell and began shooting at the dummy on the cot. As the shooter turned to leave, Sawyer fired, knocking the man back a step.

Sawyer stood from his chair, and the man brought up his gun and fired, but the hammer fell on an empty cylinder. A second shot from Sawyer's gun hit the man in the chest, causing him to fall backward against the cell bars and slide to the floor.

With the utmost caution, Sawyer picked up a lucifer and lit the lamp on the desk. He squatted and checked on the man; he was dead.

The deputy ran into the office with his gun drawn. "It looks like your plan worked. Just so you know, there's a roan with two white stockings on its right side tied up to the hitch rail out front. So I reckon this is Rufus."

"It sure seems that way, doesn't it? He figured he would kill the captain, then hightail it out of here and bushwhack me somewhere else. I would have bet money on Rufus having a partner, but he may not have had the time to hire one. Things have been happening pretty fast," said Sawyer.

"I'll go get the undertaker," said Deputy Martin. "What do you want me to do with the horse?"

"Leave it for now. I want to go through the saddlebags."

The deputy left the office, and Sawyer reloaded his gun's two empty cylinders. Then he went outside, where a dozen or so townsfolk had gathered to see what had happened.

"Sorry about the gunfire, folks. A murderer came into the jail to shoot a prisoner, and he was killed instead of the prisoner."

"Excuse me, Sheriff, is that the dead man's horse?" asked one of the citizens.

"Yes, it is. Why do you ask?"

"I work at the Ellison Hotel right over there." The man pointed up the street a half a block. "The gentleman who rides that horse rented a room this afternoon."

This was important information to Sawyer. He walked up to the hotel clerk. "What's your name?"

"It's Jeremy Long."

"Do you recall what the feller's name was?"

"Yes, sir, Dan Smith."

"Come with me. I want you to look at the corpse and see if you can identify him," said Sawyer.

"Sure thing, Sheriff."

Sawyer led the way inside the office, bent over and took hold of the dead man's hair, and tilted his face toward Jeremy. "Do you recognize this man?"

"That's Dan Smith, all right."

Sawyer stood back up. "Let's go to the hotel. I need to search his room right now."

Sawyer and Jeremy went across the street and entered the hotel.

"Give me the key to his room, and you stay here," said Sawyer.

Sawyer stood to the side of the door and turned the handle. There was no need for the key since the door ended up being unlocked. He shoved it open and looked inside to find no one in the room, and nothing but a single bed, a chair set up by the window, and a paper sack on the floor. He opened the sack, which contained nothing but chicken bones left over from someone's supper.

He left the room and went out the hotel's back door to the horse pen. It was also empty, but he couldn't distinguish how many horses had been there by the amount of horse manure and tracks, since it was too dark to tell.

When Sawyer returned to his office, the undertaker had recruited three men to help him carry the corpse to his wagon. Sawyer went inside, where Deputy Martin was cleaning the blood off the floor with a mop and a bucket of water.

"Rufus signed in at the Ellison Hotel under the name of Dan Smith. I searched his room and could tell he'd been watching us. I also found a sack with chicken bones in it. Where would he buy the chicken from?"

"That's an easy one," said the deputy. "Bertha cooks fried chicken daily at her little diner across the street from the hotel and south a block. If you talk to her, she'll remember who she sold that sack to."

"I'll have a talk with her tomorrow. I'm convinced

that the man I shot is Rufus, but I was expecting two killers instead of one, though. If Bertha identifies the dead man as the one who bought the chicken, I'll close the case."

"I'm going to dump this dirty water and go get some sleep unless you need me for anything else."

"No, you go on home, and so will I. There's nothing else we can do tonight."

Chapter Thirty-Eight

Rufus left the hotel shortly after Walter rode to the sheriff's office. He was already on his horse a block north of the jail sitting on his horse at the entrance of a side street where he had a clear view of the street and the front of the building so he could observe if Walter did his job. He made sure to position himself so he could get away if something went wrong and Walter failed his assignment. If that happened, Rufus would quietly walk his stallion north out of town and escape. The ruthless outlaw grinned as he sat on his horse and waited. Poor Walter didn't even suspect the reason behind him wanting to trade mounts. Regardless of what happened at the jail, Rufus was safe.

He saw Walter ride up in front of the sheriff's office and dismount. Walter pulled his gun from its holster and opened the door, and Rufus shook his head. They had left the door unlocked; it was a setup and this was going to end badly for Walter.

Shot after shot rang out from inside the jail. Rufus counted six in total. Maybe Walter had managed to kill the incompetent army captain after all. Then another shot sounded in the night, and then one more. Rufus grimaced in the dark. Those last two shots were from someone else's gun. Most likely, Walter was dead.

He urged his horse north along the street another block and looked back to see a crowd beginning to form in front of the jail, standing around the sheriff. How did the sheriff know they would come to the lockup after the captain? Could someone have intercepted the messages from the senator? Thinking back, Rufus decided that was how the sheriff knew to follow him to Judge Elliott's house and that he would kill Kiser.

Rufus continued walking his mount north until he cleared the buildings and houses. Then he put his heels to his horse and headed toward Iola. Or should he go to Neosho, where he could send another telegram to Senator Bass? He sure wasn't going to stay in Humboldt and go after the sheriff by himself.

He ended up riding around Iola and continuing to Neosho. At three in the morning, he came into town to find one saloon still open. He stopped his horse in front of the Ace High Tavern and went inside, where only a few customers were still drinking. He laid a dollar on the wooden counter at the bar and said, "Barkeep, bring me a bottle and glass. You make sure that the glass is clean."

"Coming right up. I'll be closing soon though, so you may want to drink up."

"Just my luck. Is there someplace I can get a room this late?"

"Yeah, the Bauer Hotel is down the street, and the front desk is open all night."

"Thanks," Rufus said, throwing back a second glass

of whiskey. "Where will I find the telegraph office? I need to send a message in the morning."

"That'll be past the hotel about a block. They're closed until eight in the morning."

Rufus laughed to himself—no telegraph office was closed to him. "Thanks." He emptied one more glass and headed back out to his horse.

He tied his horse to the hitch rail and went inside the hotel. The counter was unattended, so he slapped the bell on the counter and a few seconds later, a man came through a door to Rufus's right, carrying a bucket and mop.

Rufus reached for his gun when the door opened. "Sorry, sir, I was in the back cleaning. Would you like a room for the night?"

"Yeah, I'm kind of tired."

The man pushed the ledger book toward Rufus while he grabbed a key from the board on the wall. Rufus signed the book as John Smith.

"Your room is on the first floor, at the end of the hall. We also have a wonderful breakfast right through there in the morning," said the clerk, pointing to the doors he had come through.

"Thanks," said Rufus, and started to his room. Luckily, he was a few feet from a back door. He unlocked the latch and looked out into the alley. Excellent—there was a tiny pen for his horse. He left the door unlocked and returned to the lobby where the clerk was mopping the floor.

"I'm going to take my horse out back and put him in that pen, if that's okay."

"Of course it is. I'll open the back door, and you can come back in that way," said the clerk.

"No, you keep on with your chores. I've already taken care of that," said Rufus with a smile.

"Okay. We have oats in the barrel by the pen. You can use what you need."

"Thanks." Rufus walked outside, mounted up, and rode north for two blocks until he found the telegraph office. Once he knew where it was, he rode up the alley to the horse pen behind the hotel and took care of his horse. The walk back to the telegraph office on foot only took a few minutes. He put his shoulder against the back door and gave it a shove and the lock gave way. There was enough light from the two street-side windows for him to find the key and start tapping out his message to Kansas City.

When he was finished, he put the telegraph key back in the same position where he had found it and exited through the back door. He pulled it closed and walked to the hotel.

It would be later in the morning before he would get a reply from the senator. The telegraph office in Kansas City stayed open all night, but he wasn't sure when they would get around to delivering his message. Rufus had time to sleep before coming back to see if he had any telegrams.

Chapter Thirty-Nine

Sawyer rode out to Nancy Lou's house even though it was late, and he was tired. He had contemplated whether to stay at the hotel or ride to her house to sleep, but he knew she would be worried about him, so he'd made the ride out of town.

A huge weight had been lifted off his mind tonight. The last of his work to get revenge for the killing of their parents and her husband was all but over with. The only one left was the big boss, Senator Bass, and someone else would be taking care of him.

As he rode along the road, listening to the different sounds of bugs and critters, a feeling of relief overcame him, and he stopped his horse. Tears began to roll down his cheeks as he recalled his days on the battlefield. Even though the war is in the past, it was still a big part of his life. He could close his eyes and still visualize his fellow soldiers lying wounded, screaming in pain, missing arms or legs. And there had been so many dead bodies. At first he tried to count them but over time that wasn't an option for him.

In the first years of his service, he felt terrible and even had nightmares of the dismay that went on in battle and the awful things he had done when scouting out the enemy. He had killed with his hands, and used knives, clubs, and guns to eliminate Yankee soldiers that got in his way. He would lie awake at night and ask God to forgive him for the atrocities he'd committed. Most of the men in the opposing force didn't even know he had come up on to them. If it hadn't been war, it would have been called murder.

After the first year he learned to stuff down his feelings of guilt, fear, and horror and hide them from everyone, even himself. He would spend his downtime hiding the repulsions and terrors of what he had done and seen from his own conscience. Finally, it got to the point that he never talked to God anymore or cared what he did.

This new life had given him hope and a purpose. The wait of getting revenge was finally over, and he no longer had to kill another living soul. That made him smile as he wiped the tears from his face.

He touched his heels to his horse and continued on, thinking about brighter days. He hoped he would hear from Abe Jordan soon about the cows. Sawyer remembered the friendship, understanding, and love Abe shared with his wife Kate and their family. The night he'd eaten supper with them had been extraordinary and something that he'd needed in his battle-scarred life. They had shown him what the love between a husband and wife could look like, and the love they showed to their children gave him hope. He wanted the kind of love that they had for each other.

There were lights on in the house when Sawyer

rode into the barn. He had taken the saddle off and was rubbing his horse's back with a curry comb when Nancy came out to greet him. "Sawyer, is it over with?"

"Yeah, it is. Rufus came to the jail and filled some hay covered in blankets full of lead, thinking it was the captain. Then I killed him."

"Oh brother, I'm so glad it's over, and you're safe."

Sawyer saw the tears running down her cheeks. He put the saddle down, went to her to wipe them away, and put his arms around her. "It's going to be fine now. You wait and see. I love you, sister, and we'll make it just fine."

"I know. I'll go back to the house and warm your supper. You finish up and come on in."

Sawyer watched her exit the barn before he went back to his horse and finished caring for him. He was tired, and knew he'd sleep well that night.

When he entered the house, Nancy had a plate of food sitting on the table for him. "You go ahead and eat while I turn your bed covers down. Let's sit on the front porch and talk when you're finished."

Sawyer sat down and started eating. It must be a serious conversation she wanted to have, otherwise she wouldn't make so much of wanting to talk. He remembered growing up on the farm with her. The family sat out under a shade tree almost every evening to discuss that day's events and plan for the next day.

Nancy returned to the kitchen and washed the few dishes that were in the wash pan. Sawyer got up and brought her his plate. "That really hit the spot. I didn't realize how hungry I was until I took that first bite."

"Come on, let's go outside," said Nancy after she washed and rinsed his plate.

"What's so important that we couldn't discuss it at supper?" Sawyer said as he took a seat.

"I'm being motherly when I ask you these things, so don't get mad at me," said Nancy as she touched his arm.

Sawyer started laughing.

"What's so dad-blasted funny?" asked Nancy.

"Sister, you've been mothering me my whole life. So just go ahead and spit it out. I won't get mad."

"Well, okay then. What do you want out of life? I mean, what are your future plans?"

"I want to start a ranch on our land."

She shook her head from side to side. "No, brother, I want to know what you want out of life. Do you want to marry? Do you want ten kids? What do you want?"

Sawyer sat in deep thought for a minute or so. "When I was in Texas, I spent a little time with Abe Jordan and his wife. I saw their happiness, contentment, and companionship. But most importantly, I saw in them a unified, unselfish love for each other. I look back at our parents and see glimpses of things from their lives that I also want. Our folks worked harder than any two people I've ever seen. I know they loved each other dearly, but they didn't show that side of themselves in front of us. Very seldom did I ever see them kiss or hold hands. Rarely did I hear them say I love you to each other."

Nancy had tears streaming down her cheeks. "I'm sorry that I'm so emotional. Richard and I were in love, and we would tell each other that every day. I miss him so much at times. Don't mind me. Continue on, please."

"I'm truly sorry about Richard. I wish I'd had the time to get to know him. I haven't spent much time with

Abigail, but the few times I was around her, I had this jittery feeling in my gut. I believe it was love at first sight. I couldn't find the right words to say and felt awkward in her presence. But, sister, she made my heart flutter."

Nancy pulled a handkerchief from her pocket and blew her nose. Sawyer waited until she composed herself and reached out to take her hands into his.

"I want what you and Richard had. And what our parents had, and what the Jordans have. I want a partner and friend to be my wife until death. A house full of children is what I want. I've spent the last three years cold, hungry, and scared, and I don't want to ever kill another man. I know what my skills are, and I also know that those skills were taught to me. I'm trainable and can learn to be a better man who doesn't shoot first in a bad situation. This sheriff's job taught me that we can live in harmony and enjoy what God has blessed us with."

Nancy got up and put her arms around Sawyer's. "Thank you for sharing with me. Now it's my turn. I love Richard with all my heart and soul, but he's gone and never returning. After I have my baby, I want to find a man I can love and respect."

"After the baby is born, I'll start interviews for a new feller," said Sawyer with a grin.

"Oh no, you won't. I can do my own courting."

"Did I answer all your questions, or do you have more?" asked Sawyer.

"I do have more. First of all, when will you resign as sheriff?"

"I'll ride to Iola tomorrow and talk to the county commissioner. After that, the job will be up to the county officials. I won't quit without a replacement, and that could take about a week."

"Okay. Have you talked any more with Mr. McLaughlin about the crops?"

"No, but maybe I'll see him tomorrow."

"As soon as you hear about the cows, we need to get serious and talk about what we want to do. I suggest selling this place and buying that section south of you so we can be closer together. I still owe money on my land, but I can harvest the crop Richard planted and sell the place for way more than we gave. Then, with the profit I make off the sale of the bank, I can buy some land free and clear."

"Like I told you the other day, let's see what Abe says."

Nancy nodded. "A man from the bank in Iola is coming tomorrow to make me an offer on the bank. Do you want to meet with us?"

"Not unless you need me to. I'm confident you can negotiate with the best bankers. But right now it's getting late and I'm tired, so let's go to bed."

"You're so funny. Good night."

"Good night, sis."

Chapter Forty

The heavy footsteps of the hotel's housekeeper tromping up and down the hallway woke Rufus from a peaceful sleep. The walls in the rooms of the Bauer were so thin that he could hear the conversation of the guests next door. He threw the covers back and got up to realize it was almost noon. He needed to get dressed, find someplace to eat, and check at the telegraph office for a message.

He took his time leaving the hotel and walked outside, entering the hustle and bustle of life in the small city. Living as a faceless figure in a big city was what he preferred, instead of spending so much time on the back of a horse, traveling around the countryside.

The walk to the telegraph office gave him time to wake up from his sleep. He was grateful for the soft bed and rest, evidenced by how long he had slept.

The town marshal and another man were sitting in the lobby area inside the telegraph office while the operator was cyphering out a message coming over the wire when he walked through the door.

"Howdy." Rufus walked up to the counter. "My name is John Smith, and I'm expecting an important message from Kansas City. Have you received one for me?"

"No, sir, I haven't got any messages from there today," said the operator.

Rufus smiled. "It's still early. I'll probably get it later today." With a nod, he turned and said to the other two men, "It looks like it's going to be a scorcher out there today, doesn't it?"

"Yes it is. Are you new in town or passing through?" asked the marshal.

"Both. In fact, I'm a seed and fertilizer dealer looking for new clients. Do you own a farm, Marshal?"

"No, I don't. I'm not much into that kind of work."

With that last statement for the marshal, Rufus knew he didn't have to worry about him coming after him. The marshal was lazy and would probably turn and run in a fight.

Rufus touched the brim of his hat in a salute and went outside. So, he still had time to kill while waiting for a message. Later in the day, he'd check back. In the meantime, he would get something to eat and then have a few drinks at the saloon.

He stopped at the first café he came to. While he savored his food, he eavesdropped on the conversation a few of the locals were having. Apparently, someone had broken into the telegraph office the night before. One man said they suspected some local kids broke the lock for fun, since nothing was missing.

Once he was done eating, he walked along the boardwalk and window shopped, tipping his hat to the ladies and sometimes even smiling at them, trying to fit in with the townsfolks.

At Kaye's Emporium, he went inside and picked out a sharp-looking change of clothes. He figured the senator would want him to catch the train to Kansas City, and he wanted to look suitable for the trip. He paid for his things, went out onto the boardwalk, and found a chair to sit in and think. He still had a few concerns about the land grab operation in Humboldt. It would be a real challenge to get rid of that Sheriff McCade. Taking back the bank and other businesses could be an uphill battle since the sheriff had shown the townspeople that they could all take a stand and protect their property.

It was probably in his best interest to turn tail, leaving the lawman alone and finding another job. If killing McCade happened to go wrong, then he would be the one that died. But he had committed to working for Senator Bass, and the reward of being in charge of the senator's businesses in Humboldt could be very lucrative to him. He would wait on his instructions from the senator before he made any decisions on whether to continue to work for the senator or not. That, in itself, would be a challenge. The senator would not let him walk away since he knew all the things that the man had done.

Rufus shook off his thought, got up off the bench and took his new clothes back to his room at the hotel. After he put them away, he asked the hotel clerk, "Where can I find the barbershop, and do you have a hot bath here in the hotel?"

"The barber is almost due east behind the hotel,

and yes, we have hot baths. I can have it ready for you when you return from the barber."

Rufus smiled at the man. "Thank you so much. I'll be back shortly."

He had to wait a few minutes at the barbershop but eventually got a trim. He could afford to wait since he was killing time until he could check to see if his message had arrived.

Rufus stayed in the bathtub until his water cooled off. Piping-hot baths were one luxury he missed while away from cities. When he was home, he loved taking a hot bath every day.

Dressed in his new clothes, he stopped at the saloon long enough to have one shot of whiskey and two mugs of beer. The sun was approaching the western horizon, so it was time to return to the telegraph office.

"Howdy, sir, I'm John Smith. Did my message from Kansas City arrive?"

"Sorry, no—you didn't get a message."

Rufus nodded. "I'll check back with you tomorrow."

Something must have gone wrong. The senator had always replied to him within a few hours. Maybe he was busy and couldn't get to the telegraph office today. Whatever the reason, Rufus decided not to panic just yet. He would be patient and eat a good supper. He'd check back again tomorrow before he did anything else.

Rufus went for supper at one of the better cafés and treated himself to steak and fried taters. After that, he walked around the business section of town, wondering what to do if he found out something was wrong with the senator. He had standing instructions that if something happened to the senator, like getting arrested by the law or if he had to go into hiding for any reason, then Rufus was to go to his daughter's ranch south of Olathe, Kansas, and lay low. Rufus had only been there twice in ten years but still remembered how to get there. Even though the farm was operated by his daughter, it belonged to the senator, and no one but his close associates knew about it.

Rufus finally went to his room once it was dark. Tomorrow was a new day, he told himself, and he would wait on instructions from his boss until he was told otherwise. However, maybe this time was different and he needed a different plan. He could always send one more telegram to Kansas City before heading to the ranch. But now it was late, and time to sleep.

Chapter Forty-One

Sawyer was up at daylight and left a note on the kitchen table for Nancy before leaving the house. He wanted an early start since he planned to ride by his office to check on his deputy, and then on to Iola to talk to the county commissioner about his resignation as sheriff.

He tied his horse up in front of his office and went inside to have coffee with Deputy Martin. "Good morning, Craig. I take it that everything was quiet in town last night?" Sawyer filled a cup with scalding coffee.

"I reckon it was. Not much has happened since we elected you, Sheriff."

Just as Sawyer sat at his desk and took a sip of coffee, the door opened and the telegraph operator hurried up to his desk. "Sheriff, I got this telegram when I opened my office."

Sawyer reached out his hand. "Let me see it."

The simple message read:

Come quick to Iola, a woman murdered.

"Thanks for bringing me the message, Hank." Sawyer turned to his deputy. "Craig, there's been a murder in Iola, and I'm requested to go there."

"Do you want me to go with you?" asked Craig.

"No, Hoss will be there to help. You stay here."

Sawyer opened his bottom desk drawer, pulled out his second Colt, and buckled it onto his left hip. He had one more gulp of coffee, burning his mouth, then went outside and mounted.

He urged his horse to run down the nearly empty street, trying his best to get to Iola as quickly as he could. He slowed his horse to a lope when he could see the Neosho River in the distance to his left. He knew he was within a couple of miles from town and continued at that pace until he rode into the small city.

A dozen armed men stood in the street out front of the newly constructed sheriff's office and jail. Sawyer walked his horse through the middle of the crowd, making them give him space.

Before he could get off his horse, one man said, "We're ready to go lynch up that no-good Turner boy for what he did."

"Is that a fact?" said Sawyer as he dismounted.

"Yeah, that's a fact, and if that daddy of his gives us any problems, we'll lynch him as well."

Sawyer walked up to the man. "You do that, and I'll start one of my own. You'll be the first in line." He turned to the men. "All of you get on home or to work. This is a job for the law, and I'll not put up with lynch mobs. Now get!"

The angry man said, "Now, hold on. We just want justice done."

Sawyer spun around, and as he did, he pulled his

gun and stuck it in the man's face. "You want justice? I'll show you justice if you don't back off and let me handle this. This is your second warning. I won't give you another one."

With his eyes focused down the gun barrel, the man nodded and slowly backed away. "Come on, men, let the sheriff do his job."

Sawyer put his gun away, and as he walked toward the jail door, it swung open and Deputy Thomas came outside. He had a double-barrel shotgun in his hand, and his face was covered in sweat. "I'm sure glad to see you, Sheriff. That bunch was about to get out of hand, and I wasn't goin' to let them take over the office without a fight."

"You did good, Hoss. Now tell me what this is all about."

"A girl who sings and waits tables at the saloon was found dead early this morning in the front yard of her house. She had crawled out the door naked and covered in blood. But unfortunately, that's as far as she made it."

"What's her name?"

"She goes by Precious, but her real name is Ruth Wade. She's around twenty-three and grew up outside of town with her grandparents. As far as I know, she has no kin around here."

"So, is this Turner boy a suspect?"

"Yeah, Elenore Russel saw him and Precious walking to her house last night at about eleven. The blacksmith, Mutt Slinger, saw the Turner boy riding hard out of town this morning with blood on his shirt."

"Okay, take me to the girl's house, and we'll start there."

"We can walk there; it's only a couple of blocks.

The undertaker has probably already collected the corpse, though."

"What? How can we look for evidence if the body is gone?" asked Sawyer, with a scowl on his face. "From now on, leave the victim where you found 'em and keep everyone away from the crime scene until a thorough investigation has been done."

"Sorry, Sheriff, I ain't been around many murders before."

When they got to the house, Sawyer stopped Hoss before they entered the yard. "Point to where the woman was lying."

"She was maybe two feet from that bottom porch step. You can still see the blood on the porch from when she dragged herself outside."

"Stay here while I look around." Sawyer eased his way to the porch, then stopped, kneeled on the ground, and spent a few seconds looking at the soil. Then he rose, continued onto the porch, and entered the house. He was inside for almost ten minutes before he came back out.

"Take me to the undertaker's parlor. I want to see the victim."

"Did you find anything useful inside?" asked Deputy Thomas.

"Yeah, but let me finish my investigation before we discuss it."

The two lawmen entered the undertaker's office to find him drinking coffee.

"Come on in, gentlemen, and have a cup."

"No thanks," said Sawyer. "Have you done anything to the young woman yet?" asked Sawyer.

"Nope, I was about to get started right after my coffee. She's in pretty awful shape right now."

"Good. I want you to show me exactly how she was lying when you went to get her."

"Are you serious?"

"Yeah. Now get up, and let's get busy so I can find her killer."

The three men entered the back room, where the young woman lay on a table with a sheet over her naked body.

"If you want to see how she was lying, you'll have to help me put her on the floor. Sheriff, you lift her legs, and Hoss and I will lift her by her arms."

Once the body was on the floor face up, the undertaker placed the woman's arms out over her head. He bent one of her legs at a sharp angle and left the other leg straight.

"That's how she was lying when I got there."

"So the arms pointed toward the house, and that one leg pointed toward the street?"

"Yep. How did you know that?" asked Deputy Thomas.

"Whoever killed her dragged her by the leg out of the house and left her where she was found. She was already dead by the time he pulled her outside. From what I see by the bruising on her face and body, I would say her killer beat her and then stabbed her multiple times with a knife."

"From my experience with corpses, you are right about the beating and the knife. Precious looks to have been stabbed eight times," said the undertaker.

"I'm almost certain her attacker stabbed her outside the bedroom door," Sawyer continued. "It appears that she was trying to escape when the killer started stabbing her. The amount of blood on the floor and walls in that spot seems to support that. I also saw boot prints in the dirt where he pulled her out into the yard. Why he took her out of the house is just a guess, but I think maybe he was goin' to take the body with him to dispose of it, but something or someone frightened him away."

"I think the blacksmith was probably the one that scared him off," said Hoss.

Sawyer nodded in agreement.

"If you're through with her, can you help me put the body back on the table so I can clean her up and prepare it for burial?"

"Sure we will," said Sawyer.

When Sawyer and Hoss were back outside on the street, Sawyer said. "Hoss, go get Elenore Russel and bring her to the office. I'll go get the blacksmith. We need to get their statements on paper."

"Boss, how do you know so much about looking for evidence and figuring out what happened when you weren't even there?"

"Come back to the jail with me, and I'll tell you over a cup of coffee," said Sawyer.

When they were inside the office, Sawyer pointed to a chair. "Sit down for a few minutes and listen. I fought in the war for the Confederacy. Shortly after joining up, I was assigned to one of the units under the command of William Quantrill, although I never went on any of his raids or fought in any of his battles. His unit trained me to be a scout, and I learned skills to stay alive and track down the enemy without them seeing me. As soon as I was qualified, the army sent me to northern Arkansas, where I stayed for most of my enlistment. I saw more than my share of death and destruction. My job was to track troop movements, and once they set up camp, I had to come up with a plan of attack to relay back to my superiors. While doing my job, I often had to eliminate sentries or enemy scouts. I had to use all my skills to find and sneak up on them, because they had also been trained to be as invisible as could be. I was taught to look for the unexpected, and anything that was out of place or didn't seem right was a clue. That's the same way I looked at the crime scene and figured out what happened."

"Sheriff, it sounds like you been through the wringer and lived to tell about it. I'm glad you explained that to me. It makes sense now that I know how you were trained."

"I'm glad you understand. Now, let's get to interviewing our witnesses so we can solve this case soon."

Chapter Forty-Two

Rufus waited until he had eaten his noon meal before he went to the telegraph office again to check for a message.

"Howdy, Mr. Smith. I'm sorry, but you don't have a reply yet," said the operator.

"Okay. I'd like to send another telegram to Kansas City," said Rufus. He picked up a pencil, wrote on a piece of paper, and handed it to the operator.

To D. Stone. Where should I go?

    R. S.

"Send this to Kansas City, and I'll be back later for the reply," said Rufus and left. While standing on the boardwalk, thoughts about what could be happening swirled around in his head. It was highly unusual not to get a reply from the senator. The only thing he could come up with was that the law must be after his boss. That could be a big problem for the two of them. Rufus started walking to the horse pen behind the hotel to feed and water his horse in case he had to leave in a hurry.

He might not need a horse anymore though. What if he could take the train to Kansas City and buy another horse there and ride to the ranch? It was just a thought. He would wait on the reply to his telegram before he did anything.

After he had cared for his horse, he walked back to the telegraph office to be greeted with good news. "I have your reply message right here, sir."

"Thanks."

Rufus unfolded the piece of paper.

Kansas City is hot. Go to the ranch.

That meant the law was after Senator Bass and most likely his associates. From where the senator was, south of Olathe, Kansas, he would have a two day's ride by horse or one day if he took the train to Olathe and bought a horse there to take him to the ranch. But if the law was looking for the senator in Kansas City, they could also be looking in Olathe. So the train was out of the question. After careful consideration, Rufus decided it would be best to ride from where he was. Most likely, no one he passed on the road would recognize him.

Rufus went back to the hotel and changed into his old clothes. He folded up the new ones and put them in the packaging from the store. He'd stop at the mercantile on his way out of town, buy a bag for his things, and get some jerky and hardtack to snack on. A thought came to mind about purchasing cooking utensils and provisions, but instead he decided he would take the easier option, and take over someone's house so he could sleep in a bed and eat their food.

He left town by walking his horse until he was clear of anyone that could be watching. His plan was to try and stop somewhere close to Garnett, Kansas, for the night. It couldn't be more than thirty-five miles, and he could probably find an excellent place to hole up.

Five miles north of Neosho, his road connected with another one that ran east and west. He stopped at the crossroads, letting his horse catch his wind while he tried to decide which way to proceed. Two men came riding up behind him.

"Excuse me, but do either of you know the way to Greeley?" he asked them.

"Yep, keep going north for another ten miles and then veer off to the northeast at the Y in the road."

"Much obliged."

Rufus smiled at his good luck—it could have been hours before someone had come along. The ten miles went fast, and his horse was lathered up and winded when he came to the road he'd been told to take. The horse walked for the next mile until he came upon a creek, where Rufus stopped to let the horse have water and eat grass while he ate jerky and a cold biscuit.

When he started back out, he urged the horse to lope for a few miles before slowing him down again. It was getting dark, and he needed to watch for lights in houses set back off the road. Hardly anyone built their home close to the road out in the countryside.

Another mile down the road, he saw lights off to his right in a grove of trees. He walked his horse down the path and dismounted when he was within fifty yards of the house. The horse would be his barrier if the people in the place weren't friendly. He pulled his gun from its holster and cocked the hammer back.

"Howdy, in the house. Can I water my horse and fill my canteen from your well?" he called out.

The door opened to reveal a young man holding a pistol. "Who are you, and what do you want?"

"I'm just a weary traveler who needs water for myself and my horse."

A young woman came to the door and stood beside the man. Rufus turned his horse so that the animal was between him and the couple. When he stepped around his horse, he raised his pistol and began firing at the pair. Rufus emptied his gun and walked up to the doorway, where the couple lay dead.

Chapter Forty-Three

The blacksmith, Mutt Slinger, stopped working on a broken wagon spoke to talk to Sawyer. "I'd be glad to come to your office so you can take my statement. I know what I saw, and I'll tell you the truth."

"Thanks. Why don't you tell me what you saw as we walk toward my office? That way, you're not away from your work too long."

"You see, I came down the street that Precious lives on, and right before I got to her house, I saw someone run out of the yard and take off toward Main Street. It was so dark that I couldn't tell anything about the feller, and I didn't see Miss Precious lying in the yard."

"You never saw who came out of the yard?"

"I saw him, all right, but I didn't recognize him in the dark. I walked faster to catch up with him and saw Bishop Turner untying his horse from that hitch rail." Mutt pointed to where the man's horse had been tied.

Sawyer took four steps toward the hitch rail and looked at the tracks. "How could you tell who it was in the dark?" asked Sawyer.

Mutt pointed at the boardwalk. "By the streetlights. There are two right there where he tied his horse. It was Bishop, and he had blood all over his hands and shirt. He hopped on his horse and took off like a bat out of hell."

Sawyer stopped walking and looked at the lights and the hitch rail again. "What can you tell me about Bishop?"

"He's mean and overbearing. One time I saw him whip the town drunk, Willie, with his belt and he laughed the whole time. His daddy Chip stood by and watched the entire thing and didn't do anything to stop it. Bishop's been spoiled his whole life, never has to work, and Chip buys him anything he wants. That boy will come to town and strut around like he's better than everyone else."

Sawyer thought about this as they continued walking.

"You need to be careful when you arrest Bishop," said Mutt. "His daddy doesn't like anyone coming after his boy. In fact, old Chip will be waiting on you with his guns when you go to arrest Bishop."

When they got to the sheriff's office, Sawyer wrote down Mutt's statement and had him sign it.

A few minutes later, Deputy Thomas brought Elenore Russel in. She also gave her statement, which was in line with Mutt's, plus a few added remarks about Bishop being a smart aleck and ruffian.

"Thank you, Mrs. Russel, for your statement. It will help me to bring in the killer."

"I'm just doing my civic duty. You have a nice day, Sheriff."

"Thank you, ma'am."

When Elenore was out the door, Deputy Thomas asked, "What do you plan to do now that you know who killed that girl?"

"I'm going to the Turners' place and either arrest Bishop or kill him. It's his choice."

"I'll go get my horse. Bishop's pa, Chip ain't going to stand by and let you take his boy without a fight."

"Okay, get your horse and meet me back here."

Thirty minutes later, the two lawmen turned onto the lane that took them to the Turner house. "Hoss, you ride on the edge of the road over there, and I'll do the same on my side. I suggest you take that pistol out of your holster, cock the hammer, and be ready to shoot."

"That's probably a good idea. I'd be surprised if Chip ain't already waiting on us, primed to start shooting."

"If he is, that tells me that Bishop killed that girl. He knows that's the only reason the law would pay him a visit."

"Yeah, I totally agree," said Hoss.

Sawyer pointed to a large tree at the side of the house. "Angle over by that big oak tree and be ready for action. I'm goin' to let them know we're here."

Sawyer was riding toward the house when the front door opened to reveal a man holding a double-barrel shotgun.

"You get away from my place! You ain't taking my boy in, and I mean business."

"Mr. Turner, I'm Sheriff Sawyer McCade, and I don't scare easily. Now, since you're trying to stop me with a shotgun, that makes you an accessory to murder. I came here to arrest Bishop for the slaying of Ruth Wade. Since you know he came home covered in blood and didn't report it, I've got a good mind to arrest you."

"My boy didn't kill that soiled heifer, and he didn't come home covered in blood. Now get off my land, or I'll shoot." He raised his gun to his shoulder.

Sawyer raised his arm, fired his gun, and shot Chip Turner in the chest. The man's mouth fell open, and his eyes got big right before he crumpled to the ground.

"Hoss, ride around to the back and make it quick."

Sawyer dismounted and ran toward the house just in time to see Bishop run out the back door. Sawyer turned back around and went to his horse. He heard two shots from behind the house as he came around the corner and found Hoss holding his bloodied right arm.

"Hoss, are you hurt bad?"

"No, but he shot me in my arm."

"Where did he go?" asked Sawyer.

Hoss nodded toward a meadow behind a thin row of trees to Sawyer's left. "He ran out that way. I tried to hit him but missed."

Sawyer took off toward the meadow and saw Bishop running as fast as he could past a few grazing cows. Sawyer gained on him, and eventually Bishop stopped, bent over, and tried to catch his breath. Sawyer cocked his gun as a precaution and sure enough, his instincts were right; the young man straightened up, took aim with a pistol, and fired at him.

Sawyer held his fire until he was within fifty feet and then fired back. The first shot missed, but the second hit the man in the chest. Sawyer got off his horse and kicked the gun from the killer's hand. Bishop was still alive but in bad shape. His breath rattled in his chest, and blood was seeping from his mouth.

"Why did you kill that girl?" asked Sawyer.

"I did it for fun."

"Well, I'm going to let you die right here so you know how it feels."

Hoss walked up to Sawyer.

"Sheriff, you want me to see if I can help him?"

"No, he's done in, and a little suffering now is nothing compared to what's coming to him when he reaches Hell."

Chapter Forty-Four

Rufus saddled up his horse in the barn of the young couple. They lay in the manure-littered dirt only a few feet from him, right where he'd dropped them when he'd dragged them in the night before.

"Thanks for your hospitality. The bed and food were great," he said as he looked at their lifeless corpses. Then he walked his horse outside, mounted up, and rode away from the barn, laughing at his remarks to the stiff bodies.

He had been on the road just a short while when he entered Garrett, Kansas. It was the first town he'd come to since he left the house where he spent the night.

At the north edge of town, he stopped at a livery stable and watered his horse at the trough by the hitch rail. A man came out of the big double doors of the barn.

"How do, mister! Do you need to stall your horse?"

"No, but I would like you to give him a half-helping of oats while we rest."

"I'll be right back."

The man came back with a feed bucket that he put on Rufus's horse.

"How far is it to Olathe from here?" asked Rufus.

"It's about thirty miles, I suspect. You should make it there today."

"Thanks, here's a dollar for the feed. I'll be back in a few minutes."

Rufus got a look at two men he thought he knew as they went into a store across the street and to the south. He crossed over and removed the safety thong off his gun as he stepped upon the boardwalk. Standing just outside the store, he peered in the windows, trying to see their faces. They had their backs to him most of the time, and he couldn't get a good look at them, but they still looked familiar somehow. Something about how they walked, or maybe it was their hats and clothing.

The men paid for their supplies and turned toward the door. It was then that Rufus got a good look at their faces, and he recognized them. He turned his back to the door as the men came outside and walked south down the boardwalk.

Rufus was smiling now that he knew who the two men were. They just happened to be Sam and Joe, the two men who had robbed him in Eureka, Kansas, about a month earlier. He would give them a taste of his payback today.

The two men went down a street to the east and disappeared out of sight. Rufus followed twenty yards back and could still see them as they walked south down an alley.

Using caution as he arrived at the alley, he peeked his head around a building, but the lane was empty.

Where did they go? They had to be in one of the buildings lining the alley.

He returned to Main Street, walked south, and looked into windows along the way. Sadly, he didn't see them.

Frustrated, he turned east again and walked to the next street to check out those businesses. A small tavern was in the middle of the block, and Rufus decided to take a chance.

He eased into the place, and the stench inside almost took his breath away. Soiled sawdust covered the floor to soak up spilled liquor, tobacco spit, and vomit. He had to wait until his eyes got accustomed to the dim interior of the room, and then he saw Sam and Joe at a table on the north wall with a bottle and two glasses.

Rufus walked up to the bar. "Give me a shot of your best whiskey."

"Mister, it's all good. That'll be a dime."

Rufus took a drink and almost spit it on the floor, but that would have drawn attention to himself. Instead, he swallowed it down and turned to watch the two men.

The whiskey was burning his gut as he removed his gun from its holster and cocked the hammer back. He was about to move when the city marshal came through the door and approached the bar.

"I'll have a mug of chalk," said the marshal.

"Coming right up, Harry."

Rufus holstered his gun and said, "Barkeep, I'll also have a mug of that chalk."

When the marshal and Rufus had taken giant slugs from their mugs, the lawman turned to Rufus. "Are you new in town or passing through?"

"I'm John Smith, and I'm passing through. I've only stopped long enough to feed my horse and have a drink."

The marshal nodded and drained his glass. He waved to the bartender and said, "I gotta go."

"Where are you going?"

"I gotta go to the cemetery."

"I'm glad it's you and not me. That place gives me the creeps."

"That's a new one on me. I didn't think anything bothered you."

"It does. Come back when you're finished. I still have lots of chalk," said the barkeep.

Rufus sipped on his beer. He had seen the sign for the cemetery on the outside of town, and if he waited about five more minutes, the city lawman would be too far away to do anything when he killed Sam and Joe.

Rufus tried to be patient and continued to sip on his beer. Then, when his mug was empty, he pulled his gun, cocked back the hammer again, and walked to the table where the men sat drinking.

"Hello, boys, remember me from Eureka? I'm the man you robbed." He pointed the gun at Sam and shot him in the head. Blood and brain matter splattered onto Joe, who was caught by surprise with his mouth hanging open. Rufus turned the gun toward him and put two balls in his chest.

Rufus kept the gun in his hand until he was outside, then ran to the end of the street. Once on the side road, he ran to Main Street, walked across it to the stable, and mounted up. He rode north out of town with a smile on his face. No one robbed him and got away with it.

Chapter Forty-Five

"Hoss, can you grab that rope off your saddle? We'll drag Bishop back to the house so he can be beside his pa," said Sawyer as he walked to his horse.

"What will you do with their corpses, Sheriff?"

"I'll find something to cover up the bodies while we return to town and take you to the doctor. Then I'll notify the mortician, who can handle the bodies."

After Sawyer covered the dead men with quilts that he'd brought out of the house, he helped Hoss onto his horse. Sawyer pulled his gun, reloaded the spent cylinders, and mounted up so he could get Hoss to the doctor. They could pick up the pace if Hoss held his arm close to his chest.

Once they got back to town, the two lawmen received many looks as they walked their horses down Main Street. Sawyer took Hoss to the doctor. Then he went to the undertaker's and told him where the corpses were.

Sawyer's stomach informed him that he hadn't had

any food that morning, so he stopped at the first café he came to and ordered a plate lunch with a cup of coffee.

While Sawyer sipped his coffee, a man at a nearby table asked, "Excuse me, Sheriff, but did you arrest Bishop Turner for the death of Precious?"

"Nope. He and his pa decided to fight with Deputy Thomas and me. The undertaker is on his way to collect the bodies."

"Well, I'll be doggone. That's the best news I've heard all day. Chip Turner finally got what he deserved."

"I take it that the Turners weren't well liked in town?" asked Sawyer.

"Nope. They were the most domineering people you will ever meet. Did you find out why Bishop killed that girl?"

"Yes. Bishop said that he did it for fun."

"I don't doubt that one bit. That boy has always been a little off in the head. You enjoy your dinner, Sheriff."

"Thanks," said Sawyer, returning to his cup as he waited on his food.

Another customer said, "Sheriff, I saw you and Hoss stop at the doctor's office. Is he okay?"

Sawyer took a drink of coffee. "Hoss got shot in the arm. The doctor is patching him up. I think he'll be fine in a month or so."

The waitress brought his food to the table, and no one else bothered him while he ate his meal. The man he had talked to earlier in the café was spreading the word about the Turners.

Sawyer left the café, mounted up, and returned to

the doctor's office. Hoss had a bandage on his arm, which rested in a sling across his chest.

"Doc, is he going to be able to do his duties?" asked Sawyer.

"Yep. The bullet didn't hit any bone. In fact, it's just a flesh wound. Hoss needs to keep it elevated for a few days, and then he should be able to start using it."

"Thanks, Doc. Hoss, you can go home and follow the doctor's orders."

"Are you sure? I still have one good arm."

"I'm sure. Plus, I have something important to do at the office, and then I'm going back to Humboldt."

He rode to the office, wrote out a resignation letter on a sheet of paper, and walked to the courthouse's main entrance. Sawyer had never been inside the new courthouse and needed to figure out where to go, so he entered a door with a small sign that read, *County Clerk*. A young lady smiled as he walked up to the counter. "Hello, Sheriff. What can I help you with?"

"Can you tell me where I can find the county commissioner?"

"He has an office at the end of the hall on your right, but he might not be there. He owns and operates McDaniel Implements over by the feed mill. You might find him there."

"Thanks," said Sawyer, who tipped his hat and left the room. He went down the hall and tapped on the last door on the right before opening it. John McDaniel sat at his desk and looked up as Sawyer entered.

"Hello, Sheriff. Come in and take a load off."

"Sorry to bother you, John, but I'm here to give you notice that I'm resigning as sheriff." Sawyer handed him the letter.

"What? You can't do that."

"Sorry, but I can. I accomplished what I set out to do when I was elected. I've given my future much thought, and I want to start a cattle ranch on my family farm."

"Hmm. I appreciate all you've done, and I hope the best for you, but it also puts me in a bind as to who to replace you with. Do you have any recommendations?"

"I think Deputy Craig Martin would do a good job, and he could move to Iola."

"Okay, I'll think about that. Would you continue in the job until I hire someone?"

"Yes, I can do that. Just don't take too long."

"I hear that you killed Chip and Bishop Turner today."

"Yeah, Chip came out with a gun when we arrived at his place. He knew what his boy had done in town, but that didn't matter to him. He tried his luck but failed. Bishop tried to shoot me, and I defended myself. They're both dead."

"Those Turners have been a pain to this town for years, so good riddance."

Sawyer stood up and extended his hand. "Let me know as soon as you hire a new sheriff."

"I certainly will. In fact, I'll talk to the judge today and if he agrees with your suggestion, I'll ride to Humboldt this afternoon or first thing in the morning to talk to Craig."

"That sounds fine to me. I'll be on my way. Thanks for talking to me."

"Thank you, Sawyer."

Sawyer mounted his horse and headed back to the

Turner place. There had been cattle in the pasture where he had killed Bishop, and he wanted to have another look at them before he went back to Humboldt. If the Turners had any kin and they wanted to sell everything, he might want to buy those cows.

Chapter Forty-Six

Rufus slowed his horse down when he was five miles out from Garrett. He had a good head start on the law, and it wouldn't be but a few more miles before he came to the east road. No need to go into Olathe; he would stay south of town and go to the senator's ranch. The fewer people who saw him, the better.

He let his horse walk for five minutes, then urged him to lope for the next three miles until they came to a creek. At this stop, Rufus dismounted and led the horse down the stream so they couldn't be seen from the road. He let the pony drink his fill and tied him so he could graze while Rufus ate jerky.

After the short rest, Rufus rode the horse across the creek and stayed off the road for a quarter of a mile. When he entered the road, he again let the animal walk for a-ways, then gradually increased the speed so it would throw off anyone who tried to track him. He had learned over the past few weeks that if a horse starts running suddenly, the ground gets torn up, leaving obvious marks. But if he gradually increased his speed, it wouldn't be so obvious.

Rufus saw the east–west road that would take him toward his destination. He recognized the sign from the last time he'd been through Olathe, because the top was shaped like the roof on a barn. While keeping the pace to a lope, Rufus veered his horse east with a tug of the reins. It would be another six or seven miles before they turned south to the ranch.

Senator Bass had put the ranch in his daughter's name so no one would know he owned it. She didn't have the same last name as him and kept it quiet that he was her father. Even though he was a crook and a scoundrel, he never wanted his daughter subject to his criminal dealings. She had gone to school in Saint Louis and married a man who later got killed in battle. She kept his last name when she came back to Kansas to start over. That's when he gave her the ranch to operate.

Rufus thought he was getting close to the turnoff. He had slowed the horse to a walk and pulled his pistol to check that the cylinder was fully loaded. If something had happened to the senator in Kansas City, then there could be trouble here also, and he wanted to be ready.

A dust trail appeared off to the east, like someone was coming his way. To the left was a forest, and to the right was open meadow, so he swung his horse into the trees and waited until whoever it was passed by. It was a wagon pulled by two horses and two riders on horseback. They rode past and never looked Rufus's way.

When they were out of sight, he continued for another mile until he saw the south road. The road went directly to the ranch, and a sign about one hundred feet from the turnoff read, *No Trespassing*. The ranch house was another mile down the road and to the east about two hundred yards. Rufus rode off the road and made a broad sweep to come into the place from the barn side. He felt like there could be trouble waiting on him, and he didn't want to ride into the sights of someone waiting to arrest him or worse, kill him.

He dismounted behind the barn and left his horse tied to a tree limb. Then, with his gun in hand, he entered the barn through its back door. He took his time and looked in each stall and the tack room. No one seemed to be around. Next, he went to the side double doors and watched the house for fifteen minutes before deciding to go up to the back door.

Where were all the ranch hands? Then he remembered that instead of a bunkhouse by the barn, there was another house elsewhere on the property that housed the hired hands. The arrangement gave the senator privacy while he was here.

Rufus opened the back door of the house and crept into the kitchen. A coffee pot sat warming on the stove, next to something simmering in a large pot. He made his way to the dining room to find it empty.

A floorboard creaked in the living room. Tensed and ready for action, he stepped into the next room and a gun barrel touched the side of his head.

"I'm glad you finally made it."

"Dang, boss, you almost made me wet my pants," said Rufus.

"I saw you leave the barn and knew you would enter through the kitchen. Let's go into the parlor and have a cup of coffee. There is no one here except me, so we can talk freely."

Two cups of coffee were sitting on the table in front of the couch. When both men had sat and were sipping their coffee, Rufus asked, "What's happened to make you come out here?"

"That McCade imbecile went to Topeka and gave the US prosecutor the telegrams where I instructed you to kill the judge and ex-sheriff. McCade figured out that you broke into the telegraph office in Humboldt and sent me a message. He did that by sending out inquiries to all the stations. Now he's working with the federal authorities to incarcerate me."

"Boss, I'm sorry. I had no idea he could get to our messages."

"Don't fret about it. You and I will take care of it, and that menace will never bother me again. McCade will feel the wrath of my imposition if it's the last thing I do."

"I take it you have a plan on how we do that?"

"I'm working on it. I have someone who supplies me with information from Iola. What he tells us will direct my endeavors. For now, we'll sit tight and wait on what my informant finds out."

"That sounds good to me. I'll do whatever you tell me to do."

"I know you will. You can go ahead and take care of your horse and bring your things to the house. I'll fix us food to eat while you get settled in. Use the same room you've stayed in before."

"Yeah, that's a good idea. I left my horse tied up behind the barn. I best get him taken care of before I eat."

Chapter Forty-Seven

Sawyer was proud that he had submitted his resignation to the county officials. That was his first step in becoming a rancher and beginning the life he needed after fighting so long in the war. He could now take control of his future and do what he wanted, which didn't include the duties of a lawman. He felt like a kid again, and the world was at his fingertips.

Today he would write a letter to Abigail and tell her about his dream of the two of them becoming ranchers. He smiled. Maybe that was a bit much, but the worst she could do was tell him no, so he'd write from the heart and be as romantic as he could manage.

He had to come out of his thoughts when he saw the town of Humboldt come up in front of him. His first stop was the telegraph office to see if Abe had replied to his message.

"Good afternoon, Sheriff. I have a message for you." Mr. Hoffman handed the paper to Sawyer, who read it.

We are home. Gathered more than 3300 heads. You
have 664 cows at my place. I talked to the others.
They will sell you any amount you want and drive
for $10 a head.

> *Waiting for your reply.*
> *Abe*

"I need to send an answer," said Sawyer as he began
to write.

I will take an additional 600 heads. The terms are
reasonable. Let me know when they will leave for
Cowtown. Will meet them there. Your friend.

> *Sawyer*

Mr. Hoffman began to peck at the key and sent the
telegram. "Sheriff, would you like me to bring you the
reply when it comes in?"

"No, I'll be back later. You have a good afternoon,
Mr. Hoffman." Sawyer started to the door, very happy
to know about his cattle. As he grasped the handle, the
telegraph key began to click.

"Sheriff, it's for you."

Sawyer returned to the counter and waited until
Mr. Hoffman handed him another message.

Ronnie, Cowboy, and Hooter leave tomorrow.
Arrive in six weeks. Have money sent to the bank.

"Send another reply."

Thank you.

"Sheriff, are you going into the cattle business?" asked Mr. Hoffman.

"I sure am! In fact, I turned in my resignation to the county commissioner today."

"I, for one, thank you for what you have done for the town and me personally. I didn't know how I was going to get my business back when that crooked banker foreclosed on it without giving me notice. That bunch would have bled us all dry in time. But for my life, I still don't know why they wanted farmland."

"I don't know either, but I'm sure they had a big plan, or they wouldn't have murdered and stolen from hard-working, honest people. I'll see you around. I best be on my way."

Sawyer rode to the bank and was met on the board-walk by Nancy, smiling and dancing a little jig. She swung her arms in the air. "Little brother, I sold the bank today to the Bank of Iola."

"And that's what the dancing is all about?"

"Yes, it is. I'll turn over the operation in ten days."

"That's good news. Maybe I should take you to the café for supper tonight to celebrate our good fortune," said Sawyer, smiling.

"Oh my goodness, you really did quit your job."

"I resigned but said I'd stay a few days until the county replaces me."

"Good for you. I agree—we need to eat supper in the hotel dining room and have a big, juicy steak," said Nancy.

"You sure do like steak, sister."

"It's not me! The baby likes steak." She walked to

Sawyer and hugged his neck, even though her stomach was in the way.

When she removed her arms from around him, Sawyer put an arm on her shoulder and began to pat her back. "Sis, if you want to buy those two properties between us, then I'm in."

She looked at him and raised only one of her eyebrows. "Sawyer McCade, there's something you're not telling me."

"We have 1,264 head of cattle headed this way tomorrow from Texas. They should be here in about six weeks or so."

"Wow, I guess we're in the cattle business!"

"One other thing. I tracked down a killer this morning outside of Iola. The boy and his pa are both dead. I noticed that they were raising cattle, and I'm going back to Iola tomorrow and see if I can buy them. They look like the shorthorns I saw over by Abe's ranch when I was in Texas. He told me that a rancher can mix-breed longhorns with shorthorn cattle and raise a better grade of beef worth much more money."

"Go to the county clerk and check whose name is on the deed," said Nancy. "You can ask at the courthouse if they have any kin. Even if they did, I'm not sure they'll sell you those cows, but they may sell to someone else, and then you can buy them from that person."

"Yeah, that's a good idea. But right now I have something important to do, so I'll meet you for supper at the hotel at six."

"I'll be there. What's so important, anyway?"

"I have to write a letter."

"I've been giving that more thought too," said

Nancy. "I think it would be good if she came here. Remember to tell her she can stay with me, if she's willing to help me with this little one." She put a hand on her belly.

"Thanks, I'll be sure to let her know. See you at supper."

Chapter Forty-Eight

The evening of the day that Rufus arrived at the senator's ranch, they finished their nighttime meal, and Rufus washed the dirty dishes while the senator went into the parlor to think. That probably meant that Rufus would be told to return to Humboldt and confront the sheriff. But Rufus had left town to avoid just that; he knew he was no match for the sheriff and would need help to kill him.

When he finished the dishes and threw out the wash water, he grabbed a broom and swept out the kitchen. He was killing time so he wouldn't have to talk to his boss.

"Rufus," he heard his name called out. "Let whatever you're doing go, and come on in here."

A half-empty bottle of whiskey and two full glasses were sitting on the table in the center of the room. "Have a seat, and explain to me everything you know about McCade."

Rufus began his story, starting with when he and

Avery arrived in Humboldt and finished with how Walter walked into the jail to a setup.

The senator sat in his chair and said nothing for a few minutes. Then he said, "That makes me surer than ever that we've got to sit tight till we hear from my man in Iola. That will also give the sheriff more time to cool off and think he's in the clear. You'll stay here with me, and when we get an update from my informant, we'll devise a plan to kill the sheriff and get my bank back."

"I could use some rest to work the soreness out of my butt, thanks to that saddle."

"I'm not concerned about your butt," said Senator Bass. "However, this is how we will coexist while we're together. I hate to wash dishes, so if I cook, you can clean."

"Fine by me. I'm a terrible cook anyway," said Rufus.

"Tomorrow, I'll need you to ride into Olathe and go to the telegraph office. Use the name Ed Johnson and check for messages. No one there will suspect anything since you're a stranger and I'm not with you, so it should be fine."

"Okay. Should I leave here right after dinner?"

"Sure, or maybe around two o'clock; it shouldn't take more than an hour to get there and back."

Rufus got up and set his empty glass on the table. "I left my horse in a stall to eat his oats. I'm goin' to turn him out into the horse pen for the night. Is there anything you need while I'm outside?"

"Yes, bring in an armful of firewood for the kitchen stove. I'll cook flapjacks for breakfast."

"That sounds good."

Rufus took his time in the barn, and when he came

back to the house, the senator wasn't in the parlor and the whiskey bottle was empty. His boss must have retired for the night. Rufus headed to his room and went to sleep as well.

After breakfast the following day, the senator wanted to talk while they ate.

"Some say that land will be worth a lot of money in just a few years," he said. "When we secure the bank operations again, I want to acquire as much land as we can get our hands on. You'll be the bank president and loan as much money as possible to the farmers in the county."

"Let me get this straight," said Rufus. "I loan them money and make them put up their land as collateral. When they can't pay, then we can take it from them, or we can use the loan to make them do what we want."

"You're catching on fast," said Senator Bass. "Either scenario will benefit us and make us rich men."

"Don't you think that we're getting ahead of ourselves? We've got to kill the sheriff before we can do anything."

The senator slammed his open hand on the table. "I realize that!" he shouted at Rufus. "He's a real sore in my side, and I want him dead."

Rufus didn't want to be anywhere near his boss when he was in a bad mood. He wanted to get away from him.

"I want him gone also. I should catch my horse and get him ready to ride into town. I think I remember how to get there, but I'm not real sure."

Senator Bass had a blank look on his face, and his eyes seemed to be sunk back in their sockets. He got up and walked to the kitchen window before looking back at Rufus. "All you have to do is follow the signs along the road," he said in an almost whisper.

"Oh, I didn't know there were signs," said Rufus as he got up and started out the door. Something was bad wrong with his boss. It seemed like the man was obsessed with killing the sheriff and getting his bank back. The old coot ought to cut his losses and move on, but as long as he paid Rufus a good salary, he'd do whatever his boss wanted.

Rufus spent the next two hours killing time in the barn to stay away from Bass. When he thought the senator had time to cool off and hopefully had returned to his right mind again, Rufus got his horse ready and led him to the house, where he tied him to the hitch rail close to the back door. He went in and sat at the table with the senator to eat a meal before he started to town. A bucket of unshelled field peas rested on the table in front of the senator waiting to be snapped. He was deep in thought with a pea pod in his hand, staring off into nothing.

Rufus asked, "Are you shelling those peas so we can have them for supper tonight?"

The senator jerked his head up and put the bucket on the floor. "Yeah, I'm working on that, but I have other things on my mind right now."

Rufus left well enough alone and got up and went to the stove. He filled himself a plate of ham and potatoes that the senator had made while he was in the barn.

Senator Bass also got up to get himself some food.

When Rufus was finished eating, he pushed his chair back. "I'm heading into town. Is there anything I can pick up for you?"

"Why are you going into town?" asked the senator, sounding confused.

"I have to check on your messages at the telegraph office."

"Oh yeah, I forgot. Remember, your name is Ed Johnson."

"Yes, sir, I got it."

Rufus was glad to get away from the house. The senator seemed to be losing his mind. He was in his seventies, and maybe old age was making him that way. The senator's demeanor made Rufus uneasy since the man was so adamant about killing the sheriff. If the senator wasn't thinking straight, it could be deadly for both of them. Rufus decided to kill an hour at the saloon while he was in town, to avoid spending so much time alone with the old man.

He took his time getting to Olathe by letting his horse walk most of the way. He went to the telegraph office first, and there happened to be two messages waiting on him.

Sheriff resigned today. Buying cows.

Rufus thought about what this meant. Sheriff McCade must have figured that he'd killed Rufus and all his troubles were over. That might make him easier to bushwhack since he had let his guard down. Rufus opened the second message.

The bank was sold today. The new owner is the Bank of Iola.

This last message might make the senator blow his

top, Rufus thought. Or it could be a relief to him. He had said that his informant was in Iola. Maybe it was the banker.

He folded both messages and put them in his pocket. These telegrams were good news, and he wanted to get them back to the senator. Good news might make the old man start thinking with his right mind.

Chapter Forty-Nine

Sawyer struggled with what he wanted to say to Abigail but finally wrote down what he deemed to be a love letter. It was the first actual letter he had ever written. With his declaration of love in his pocket, he walked to the mercantile, where the post office occupied one of the back corners.

"Ma'am, I'd like to send this letter to Clarksville, Texas."

"Sheriff, you first need an envelope and an address where to send it. I have envelopes if you want to buy one for a penny."

"Yes, ma'am, I want one, but I don't know her last name or address. What can I do so she'll get it?"

"Do you know where she works?"

"Yes, she's a waitress at the Main Café on Main Street in Clarksville, Texas. Her name is Abigail."

"I'll help you out and address the envelope for you. Do you have a mail slot here at the post office or in town somewhere?"

"No, ma'am, I don't get mail. However, you can put my address as the sheriff's office."

"Your address will be general delivery, Humboldt, Kansas."

"Thank you, ma'am," said Sawyer and paid her what he owed.

When he left the store, he saw Owen Potter, the carpenter who was supposed to give him an estimate on his house and barn, go into the gun and leather shop. Sawyer walked that way since he was early for supper with Nancy and had some time to kill.

When he entered the gun shop, Owen had a rifle against his shoulder and looked down the barrel at Sawyer. "Hey, Sheriff," he said.

"Hello. Have you put together a cost for my building projects?"

"I've got one for the house, and I'll be finished with the one for the barn by tonight. I can bring them to the jail first thing in the morning."

Sawyer had his eyes on several pistols in the glass-fronted display case. "That'll be just fine." He pointed to a short-barrel gun in the case. "What kind of gun is that?" he asked the shop owner, who stood behind the counter.

"That's a new .31 caliber Colt pocket gun that uses cartridges instead of cap and ball, although a man would need a deep pocket to carry it. Businessmen carry one in a shoulder holster, so it's not easily seen," said the shop owner.

"What do you mean by shoulder holster?"

"I have one right over here. Let me get it, and I'll strap it on you if you'll remove your vest."

The man put the contraption on Sawyer, slid the

Colt in it, and Sawyer put his vest back on. "Well, I'll be. That hardly shows at all," said Sawyer as he looked into a mirror mounted on the wall. After removing his vest again, he pulled the rig off and handed it back to the man. "How much do you want for the gun and holster?"

"I'll take thirty-six for both of them."

"I'll think about it. I need to go now. I have a supper date with my sister and can't be late."

"You think it over about the gun."

"I certainly will. By the way, what's your name?"

"I'm Albert Van."

"Okay, thanks, Albert. I'll get back with you on the gun." He turned to Owen, who had put the rifle down and was looking at tool belts hanging on a peg. "I'll see you in the morning, Owen," said Sawyer.

"Yes, sir, I'll be there."

Sawyer left the shop and hurried down the boardwalk because it was time to eat.

The hotel dining room was crowded with people having their evening meal. Sawyer and Nancy kept their conversation to everyday things concerning the town, keeping their ranching plans to themselves.

When they finished eating and went outside, she said, "We need to go somewhere private and talk."

"We can go to my office. Deputy Martin has left for the day, and no prisoners are occupying the cells."

Once inside, Sawyer let Nancy sit in his chair while he sat on the edge of the desk. "So, what do we need to talk about?"

"I saw Mr. Tomlinson, who owns the land between my place and our home place, in the bank this afternoon and made him an offer. I didn't know this until I talked to him, but he owns both sections we want to buy. Phil Paisley, who is on the section closest to our family land, only sharecrops that portion with Mr. Tomlinson. I made Mr. Tomlinson an offer of seventeen dollars an acre. He countered back." She sat smiling at Sawyer.

"Well, don't keep me in suspense. What was his counter?"

"He has one hundred and twenty cows, five bulls, and forty calves, and he'll take nineteen dollars an acre for the land and cattle. So that comes out to $24,320 for the land and cattle. We can go in together and buy him out. What do you think about it?"

"It's a fair price, and I can afford my half. Although I still have to pay for the extra cattle coming from Texas. What about the houses on the property? Did you ask what kind of shape they're in?"

"Yes, I did. I can move into Phil's house—it's in good shape. And you can remodel the other house much cheaper than having someone build you a new one at our parents' place. He also said that both properties have large barns and chicken pens."

"This is good! I'm still planning to inquire if we can buy those cows at the Turner place. I'll take your advice and see if the county commissioner will strike the deal, if they have any relatives that want to sell," said Sawyer.

"You do that. I'll give you the money for my half of the cattle coming up from Texas, and if you can make a deal on the Turner cattle, I can pay my part of that as well."

"You must have made a good profit on the sale of the bank."

"You might say I did really well."

"I'm proud of you. Will you spend the night in town or go to your house?"

She thought for a few seconds before answering. "I think I'll spend the night in town. It's late, and I don't want to ride alone to the farm."

"If you want to go home instead, I'll go with you and keep you safe from the bogeyman," said Sawyer, laughing at the look on Nancy's face.

"Oh my goodness, I haven't heard that word in years. Okay. Come on, let's go home."

Chapter Fifty

The day following his trip to Olathe, Rufus was in no hurry to get out of bed and talk to Senator Bass. After he was dressed, he began to smell bacon cooking and went to the kitchen to find the table set, with coffee in the cups and a platter of bacon, cathead biscuits, and fried eggs.

"Do you expect company for breakfast? There's enough food for a small army on the table," said Rufus.

"That's not all. I still have gravy on the stove. I'll get it, and then we can discuss my plan while we eat."

"That's fine by me," said Rufus as he sat down and grabbed two biscuits.

Senator Bass put a gravy bowl on the table and smiled as he filled his own plate. Rufus watched him and thought the man seemed in a much better state of mind and spirit than the day before. Did the news about the sheriff have anything to do with it?

The senator ate his food, and when his plate was empty, he pushed it aside, picked up his coffee cup, and blew on the hot liquid before he took a sip. Although it had cooled off some while he ate, he did it out of habit. "I've studied those telegrams, and I think the sheriff figured that he killed you. He thinks that he and the government have wiped out my operation. That's given him a false sense of security, and we will use that to eliminate him."

"Just how are we going to do that?"

"You and I will leave for Humboldt the day after tomorrow by horseback. We'll ride into town, and I'll acquire us lodging. You've been there before, and I don't want anyone to recognize you. After that, I'll execute my grand plan to show the citizens of Humboldt that no one is out of my reach. We'll assassinate McCade right in the heart of town. Then there will be no one that can stop us."

"I have concerns about confronting him in town. He's already killed seven men that I know of. Do you mind telling me this grand plan that you have?"

"Simple. We watch the street, and when he's not expecting it, we come up behind him and force him into an alley. Then, we fill him full of lead and leave him for dead. After we kill him, we go to the bank and buy out whoever bought it from his sister. And as for his sister, I will put a bullet in her too."

"It seems like you've put a lot of thought into this plan, and you know what? It just may work. I like the idea of sticking a gun in his back and taking him to an alley," said Rufus as he leaned back in his chair with his arms crossed, smiling.

"Go to the barn and give our horses a big helping of oats and check them over thoroughly; the last thing we need is a horse to go down on us," said the senator, clearing off the table.

Rufus grabbed his hat and went to the barn to do his chores. It seemed that the senator had gotten his right mind back. Rufus could see a significant change in him since the day before. He hoped his boss would keep his wits when they got to Humboldt, or they'd both end up dead.

A tin of saddle soap and a pile of rags sat on a shelf by the saddle tree. An idea came to Rufus that would keep him busy for a while. He started applying the soap to the leather on his saddle. He used his hand to rub the treatment into the leather and wiped off any excess with a rag. When he finished his saddle, he did the same to the one that Senator Bass used.

Rufus then rummaged around inside the feed room and found a small burlap sack that would be perfect for storing a couple of helpings of oats for the horses. They'd need food when they stopped for the night on the journey to Humboldt.

He finished in the barn and returned to the house, where the senator was seated at the kitchen table with his gun taken apart. He was cleaning each piece with a rag soaked with gun oil.

Rufus went to the stove, took a rag to hold the handle of the coffee pot, and poured himself a cup. "I fed the horses well, and I'll bring a sack of oats with us on the trip. I also cleaned and treated both our saddles. Can you think of anything else we'll need along the way?"

"I wanted to talk to you about our accommodations. Unfortunately, I'm not familiar enough with the towns we travel through to know if there are hotels along the route," said the senator as he put the pieces of his gun together.

"We can find plenty of good places to sleep. I usually find a farmhouse and take it over for the night."

"What about the people who live there?"

"I kill them."

The senator spun the cylinder on this gun and looked down the barrel. "All right, that would be fine as long as there isn't anyone left who can identify us."

Chapter Fifty-One

Sawyer was sitting at his desk the following day after he had written the letter to Abigail, holding a cup of coffee, when Owen Potter entered the office.

"Good morning, Owen. Hot enough out there for you?"

"My goodness, yes," said Owen, wiping sweat from his forehead.

"Grab yourself a cup of coffee, and then I'll update you on some changes I've made to the plans for my house."

"Sure thing. I'm curious about your changes. They could affect my estimate."

Sawyer waited until Owen had sat down to start talking. "I'm going to move into the house where Mr. Tomlinson lives, and my sister, Nancy, will move into the house where Phil Paisley lives. I would like you to remodel her house first and then mine. I still want you to clear off the debris where our homeplace burned down."

"Wow, that is quite a change. Are both houses currently occupied?"

"Yes, but they won't be for long. I'll set it up with Mr. Tomlinson for you to look them over so you can make arrangements for the materials."

Three shots rang out from someplace north of the jail. Sawyer stood up and went to the door. "I have to go."

He ran out to the street and saw some men in the middle of the road about a hundred feet north of the jail. One had a gun and wore only his britches and hat. The other four were men from town who worked in shops along the street. Sawyer ran toward him, and the man pointed his weapon in Sawyer's direction.

Sawyer stopped. "Hold on, partner, what's the matter?" He took a cautious step closer.

"I'm sick and tired of people mistreating me, and I'll kill the next man who laughs at me."

Sawyer saw Deputy Martin coming up behind the man. "Roy, put that gun down. You're drunk," said the deputy.

Roy turned to point the gun at the deputy, and that was when Sawyer stepped in and hit the drunk in the back of his head with the butt end of his weapon. The morning excitement was over.

"Y'all go on about your business," said Sawyer to the folks who were watching.

He and Deputy Martin took Roy by his arms and dragged him to the jail so he could sleep off the liquor in a cell.

Owen was on his second cup of coffee by then. "Are you sure you want to give up the sheriff's job? You handled that pretty well."

"I didn't come back from the war to be a lawman who could kill or be killed at any time. Instead, I want to forge out my destiny and pursue my dream of being a rancher."

"I totally understand where you're coming from. I couldn't wait until I could be my own boss. Well, I have work to do, so I'll be on my way now. Let me know when I can go look at those houses."

"Okay, thanks. I'll get with you soon."

Sawyer turned to Deputy Martin. "I have some things to do, so I'll be gone for a while."

"Not a problem. When I finish this cup of coffee, I'm going to make my rounds in town and look in on the businesses, so they know we're doing our jobs. And I almost forgot, the county commissioner told me via telegram that he would be here today at two, and wants to talk to me."

"That's good. I hope he offers you the job of sheriff."

"He might be wanting to tell me that he's hired someone else."

"I doubt that. You be ready to give John an answer when he gets here. I'll see you later."

Sawyer walked to the gun and leather shop, where he had looked at the gun and holster the day before. When he entered the store, the owner reached into the gun case and brought out the Colt pocket pistol.

"Here you go, Sheriff. Feel the balance of it?"

"Yeah, it feels just fine. I've thought it over and want it and that rig you put on me yesterday. I no longer have to haul around all my pistols when I'm in town. This hidden one should be all I need unless I'm in the pasture with my cattle. Then I'll carry the one on my hip."

"Yes, sir, I'll get the shoulder holster fitted on you, and I can adjust the straps. Do you plan on wearing a vest or coat most of the time?" asked the man.

"Since the temperature will change soon to fall temperatures and then winter, I'll buy another vest and maybe a dress jacket in town. Although it's funny, I've never owned a dress jacket my entire life."

Sawyer practiced taking the shoulder rig on and off a few times to get used to doing it himself. "I think I can maneuver it now. If you don't mind, could you package that up, so no one will know what it is? Then I'll go to the store and buy myself a new vest and jacket. I would also appreciate it if you wouldn't tell anyone about me buying this."

"I'll not tell a soul."

"Thanks. Go ahead and put in two hundred rounds of cartridges. I'll need to target practice with that short-barrel until I'm comfortable with it."

"Sure thing. How about you go to the store, buy your jacket, and then return here to put the holster and gun on? That way, no one will wonder what you bought from me if they happen to see you leave. I'll have your other things boxed up, and your bill figured when you return."

"That sounds good to me," said Sawyer, and he left.

He walked to Adam's Mercantile to look for jackets. "Hello, Mr. Adams. I want to buy a dress jacket. Do you have anything like that?"

"No, I have winter coats but not dress jackets. But I know who does. Three doors down at the dress shop, Martha has a good selection of fancy clothes for men."

"You don't say! I didn't know she carried men's clothing, but then again, I never needed a nice jacket before. Thanks a lot."

Sawyer started to leave, but Mr. Adams put a hand on Sawyer's shoulder. "Sawyer, I want you to know that I appreciate you, and I hope your cattle operation goes well. I hate that you won't be our sheriff, but you'll still be a part of this community."

"Thanks for the kind words, Mr. Adams."

Sawyer bought a single-breasted black jacket that came to his mid-thigh in the dress shop, along with a new linen shirt and string tie. He put on the jacket and took the other items to the sheriff's office so he wouldn't have to carry them around town as he continued his errands.

When he entered the office, there sat John, the county commissioner, and Deputy Martin. "Hello, John. Have you hired a new sheriff?"

"I have. Meet Sheriff Craig Martin."

Sawyer walked over to Craig, pulled the sheriff's badge off his own shirt, and said, "Stand up. I'd like the privilege of pinning this badge on you, Craig."

"Thanks, Sawyer. I wouldn't want anyone else to do it."

Sawyer pinned the badge on his former deputy. "Congratulations, and you know I'll have your back anytime you need it."

"Thanks, Sawyer. I'll do my best to uphold the law."

"I know you will." He patted Craig on the shoulder, then turned to John. "You made a good choice today. And now that that's done, I have another matter to discuss with you."

"Okay, I'm here as long as you need me. What is it?"

"I saw some cows at the Turner place that I want to buy. Did Chip have any relatives that will take over his place?"

"He has a daughter who lives in Iola, but she always claimed not to know Chip or Bishop. There was bad blood between them. In fact, she didn't even go to the cemetery when the undertaker buried her kin. Her name is Faith Robbins. I've known that family for years, and I can talk to her about selling the cows if you want me to, but don't get your hopes up with her. Like I said earlier, she disowned them and may not want anything they have."

"I understand if she doesn't want to do anything with them. But please let her know that someone needs to take care of them, whether that's me or someone else. I do appreciate that you're willing to ask her. If she does want to sell, I'll pay her a fair price."

"I'll go see her today and send you a telegram about what she says."

"Thanks a lot." Sawyer patted the new sheriff on the shoulder a second time. "I'm going to leave you two so you can finish your business."

"Thanks, Sawyer. You know there's always hot, strong coffee here for you anytime you're in town," said Sheriff Martin.

"I know, thanks. I'll check in soon and watch for that telegram, John."

Sawyer took his package with him since he wasn't the sheriff anymore and returned to the gun shop. There, he put on his new holster and gun and removed the one on his hip so Martin could put it in the box with his ammo. Then, he left and walked to the bank with his package under one arm and the box in the other.

Nancy happened to be in her office with the door closed when Sawyer arrived. He went up to the counter, and the clerk greeted him. "Good afternoon, Sheriff."

Sawyer smiled at him and said, "I'm not the sheriff anymore. Craig Martin is the new sheriff. Is Nancy busy in her office, or is she napping?"

The clerk laughed. "Oh no, sir, she never takes naps. She's in there with the new owners of the bank. If you want, I can announce that you're here."

"That won't be necessary. I'll do it myself. Nancy wants me to meet them."

Sawyer tapped on her door. He heard her call out to come in and opened the door to find her and three men seated in chairs around her desk.

Nancy stood up and said, "Gentlemen, this is my brother Sawyer, and he and I are in the cattle business."

Sawyer went to each man and shook hands. "It's nice to meet you fellers. Are you the bank's new owners, or are y'all still in negotiations?"

One of the men acknowledged the question. "Yes, I do believe that we've come to an agreement."

"Sawyer," said Nancy, "we have come to an agreement with one small stipulation. They want your word that you will continue to do business with the bank and let them handle your money."

"Before we get to that, I want to let you men know I'll be spending a good portion of my funds on cows and land. So until we start selling cattle, my account will be down from where it is now. If that's still fine with you, the McCade Cattle Company will continue using this bank."

All the men nodded in agreement. Sawyer set his box and package in the corner of the room. "Well, I only came by to leave a few personal items here until I go home. It was nice meeting all of you, and I look forward to working with you in the future."

"Bye, brother. I'll see you at home tonight," said Nancy as Sawyer shook hands with the bankers again.

Sawyer turned and as he started to leave, he heard Nancy say to her guests, "Give me one minute to tell my brother something."

Sawyer went outside the bank and waited. She must have wanted to tell him something important, or she wouldn't have excused herself.

She joined him on the boardwalk. "I bought the two sections from Phil this morning. The deeds are at the courthouse, and I'll pick them up later today. Phil said you can come by anytime to look the houses over."

"That's good. I'll let the carpenter know so he can go with me. John McDonald will help us try to buy the Turner cows. I should know something later today."

"Okay, I better get back inside. By the way, you look very nice."

He smiled and walked off.

Chapter Fifty-Two

After two days of traveling, Rufus and Senator Bass were close to Humboldt. The senator was not used to riding a horse for long hours and complained to Rufus that his butt was sore and his back hurt. Rufus wished the senator had stayed at the ranch, but he knew the old man wanted in on the kill.

"Senator, we're within a half mile of Humboldt."

"All right. Is there a side street close to the hotel where I can dismount and let you take my horse with you?"

"Yeah, I believe it's called Wheat Street and it's south of the hotel about a block away."

"Good. I'll walk from there to the hotel, and I'll get us two rooms while you tend to the horses. I want a hot bath in hopes it soothes my back. You can do the same or scout the town; it's your choice."

"I'll take care of the horses and then go by the saloon to see if I can overhear what McCade is up to. Hopefully I can find out where he stays at night. We can eat supper when I return, if you're up to it."

Rufus led the way, and they split up once they turned down Wheat Street. The senator walked down the boardwalk and entered the front of the building to rent them some rooms, while Rufus took care of the horses out back. Rufus had unsaddled the horses and turned them into the pen when the senator came out of the back door, walked to the lot, and handed Rufus his room key.

"We're upstairs in adjoining rooms that face the street. The clerk is heating my bath water, so I'll see you shortly."

"Yeah, you go ahead and take your bath. Leave that back door unlocked when you go back in. I'll come in that way."

Before the senator could get to the back door, it swung open, and the clerk hollered, "Sir, your bath is ready in room ten."

The clerk moved out of the senator's way as he went back into the hotel, and then closed the door behind them. Rufus hoped he hadn't been recognized, but the clerk probably didn't remember when he'd been there with Avery almost a month ago. Plus he now sported a full beard and that would make it difficult to see his face. The hotel clerk didn't show any signs of remembering him. In fact, he hadn't even looked twice at Rufus.

Rufus walked down the alley to the street, then headed to the saloon and took a table in the middle of the action so he could hear everyone's conversations. He was in no hurry to return to the hotel to listen to his boss complain about his back and butt hurting.

He sat and sipped his beer, listening to the men at the table beside him. After a few minutes, one of the men mentioned that McCade was not the sheriff anymore and that Deputy Martin had taken his place. Another man said that he heard McCade and his sister bought land to start a cattle ranch.

Rufus wanted to ask questions but kept quiet. The conversation then mentioned how McCade had single handed eliminated the criminals that had taken over the town. One of the men said something about him having cattle being delivered from Texas. Rufus turned his attention to the other tables but noting else was said about the ex-sheriff.

Chapter Fifty-Three

The hotel clerk opened the door of the sheriff's office and stuck his head inside, where Sawyer and Sheriff Martin sat in conversation. Sawyer hadn't intended to go back to the office today, but Sheriff Martin had flagged him down when he left the bank earlier. The sheriff motioned for the clerk to come on in. "What can I do for you?" he asked.

"I came to tell Sawyer that a well-dressed elderly gentleman just checked into the hotel and rented two rooms. He's got another man with him outside putting up the horses, and I don't think that other feller wanted me to see him. I remember him from when he was here about a month ago. He was with that feller you killed out on the road close to the judge's house. You know, the same one who robbed the bank."

Sawyer asked, "Are you saying Rufus is at the hotel?"

"He's not there right now, but he has a room. I watched him through the back window, and he went to the Star Saloon. But the older gentleman is at the hotel in the bathtub."

"Thanks, I really appreciate this information," said Sawyer. "What are their room numbers?"

"They are on the second floor in rooms three and five," said the clerk.

"What was the man who went to the saloon wearing?"

"He has on a striped shirt. It's brown and gray and he has a full beard, He is also wearing a cowboy hat this time and not a bowler hat."

"Okay, you best get back to the hotel in case they need you for something," said Sawyer.

"Yes, sir. You take care," said the clerk.

When the clerk was gone, Sheriff Martin asked, "How do you want to handle this?"

"I don't want you involved this time. You're the sheriff, and I hate you getting caught up in my fights. I'm going to the saloon to confront Rufus, and then I'm goin' to the hotel for the other one."

"Do you know who the older feller is?" asked the sheriff.

"I suspect that it's Senator Bass, and he's here to personally see me dead, but that's not going to happen. I'm fed up with him and his murderous gang. Craig, I've been on the run for the past three years fighting in the army, and I'm done with all that. Now this is in my hometown, and I'll end this thing today and get on with my life."

"I respect your judgment, Sawyer. I'll walk down the street to the hotel to make sure the older gentleman doesn't leave before you get to him. You go do what you have to do."

"Thanks."

Sawyer entered the saloon and spotted a man wearing a brown and gray striped shirt sitting alone at a table. It had to be Rufus—he was the only man with a striped shirt and beard in the whole place. Sawyer walked up to the bar counter and ordered a beer. He made sure he could see Rufus in the mirror behind the bar.

Sawyer knew by the smile on Rufus's face that he had recognized him when he took his place at the counter. Once he had his beer, Sawyer never took his eyes off the mirror.

With his left hand, he lifted his mug and saw Rufus reach to his side and take his gun from its holster. Sawyer reached into his coat, pulled the pistol, and held it close. Rufus was within two steps when Sawyer turned and fired, shooting Rufus in the abdomen. The wounded outlaw dropped his gun and went down to his knees. Sawyer knocked Rufus's hat off and grabbed a handful of the man's hair.

"We can end this right now, or you can tell me what I want to know. If you cooperate, I'll get you a doctor."

Rufus was going fast, still on his knees but struggling to stay alive—his breathing was raspy and blood began to flow out both corners of his mouth. He began to gasp for air. Sawyer knew he only had a little time. "Is Senator Bass at the hotel?"

Rufus smiled, and now blood flowed from his nostrils as well as his mouth. He reached out and pulled his gun toward him for one last attempt to fire. Sawyer shot him again, and he was dead.

Sawyer reloaded his gun and slid it back into his holster. He picked up Rufus's gun and tucked it into the waistband of his britches. "One of you men go tell Sheriff Martin that Rufus is dead, and he'll notify the undertaker."

"Yes, sir, I'll go," said a man in overalls..

Sawyer walked down the boardwalk to the hotel. When he entered the lobby, the clerk pointed upstairs and held up three fingers. Sawyer eased his way upstairs until he came to room number three and tapped on the door.

"Boss, are you in there?"

The door opened, and Sawyer shoved the man back into the room. He pulled Rufus's gun from his waistband and placed it on the bed.

"Senator Bass, I'm Sawyer McCade, and I'm here to end this between you and me. You may not know this, but I take no prisoners. I'm giving you a fighting chance, so pick up that gun, and we end this here and now." Sawyer pulled his coat back to expose his gun in the shoulder holster.

"Where's Rufus?" asked the senator as he moved closer to the bed.

"He's dead. Go ahead and pick up that pistol because I'll kill you one way or the other. Like I said, you'll not walk out of this room, ever!"

"Look, I'm a harmless old man, and I'm sure not a gunfighter. I'm a businessman, and if you join me, we can accomplish great endeavors together. I know the most influential politicians and businessmen in the state of Kansas and Missouri. So you partner with me, and I can make you a wealthy man, Mr. McCade."

"You've already made me a rich man, senator. I'm the one who robbed your money from the bank the first time."

Sawyer could tell he'd pushed the crook's right button. The man's face turned red and his hand started shaking.

Sawyer watched Senator Bass extend his left hand toward the gun on the bed, but while doing so, he also raised his right hand, which held a two-shot derringer. Sawyer pulled his gun from his shoulder holster and fired once. The late Senator Bass fell dead on the floor with a bullet hole in his forehead.

Sawyer placed his gun in its holster and looked down at the lifeless corpse on the floor. He had cut the head off the snake, and it was finally over. He closed his eyes and thanked the Lord for watching over him.

A Look at Book Three

A Rancher's Revenge

He came home to start over. But trouble came first.

Sawyer McCade came up hard, shaped by war and trained to kill as a soldier for the Confederate Army. But those days are behind him now. Sawyer returns to Kansas with one goal—build a quiet life as a rancher. The land is ready, the cattle are coming, and a woman from his past may just make it all complete. For the first time in years, the future looks promising. But trouble finds him fast.

When word reaches him that the herd—and the men driving it—have been ambushed on the trail, Sawyer is forced to saddle up once more. Outlaws and Apaches hold the key to his future hostage, and justice isn't coming unless he delivers it himself.

With everything he's worked for hanging in the balance, Sawyer must walk the line between the life he wants and the man he used to be.

Will he find peace at the end of the trail, or lose himself to the fight once more?

AVAILABLE AUGUST 2025

About the Author

Monty was born and raised in Southeastern Oklahoma in the small town of Sawyer, which is nested along the banks of the Kiamichi River. He's owned horses and cattle, riding the former and working the latter. Over the years, he formed a deep connection and respect for the Old West and the courageous folks who braved the wild frontier.

Monty is an avid reader and is particularly enthusiastic when it comes to Western authors and novels. His love of reading sparked his desire to write his first short story. He loves writing about real places and landmarks from the 1800s. In college, he wrote a ten-page paper about his grandmother, born in 1886, who married at fourteen and took in five orphaned nieces and nephews shortly thereafter. Monty's love for history and penchant for storytelling earned him an A+, and he hasn't looked back since.

Now retired, he loves to travel, fish, spend time with his four grandkids, and tell stories. He looks for inspiration for future books wherever he goes, and he is a member of the Western Writers of America Inc.

www.montygarnerauthor.com